"Is there an
make you more comfortable?"

"Well," James sighed, "you could come over here and give me the comfort of your cool hand on my fevered brow."

"Apart from being tempted to slam an ice bag on your so-called fevered brow, James Linklater," Polly retorted, catching the glint of amusement in her patient's eyes. "I think you are trying to bamboozle me."

"Perish the thought!" James protested. "You see before you a grievously ill man, alone among strangers, wanting only some small crumb of comfort. But what does this hard-hearted woman offer him? A damned ice bag!"

"Okay, okay—I get the message!" Polly giggled. "So, what do you really want? Within reason," she added quickly.

"Surely all is reason when two hearts beat as one!" James grinned wolfishly.

Polly laughed aloud, ridiculously happy. And in that instant she knew how less vibrant life would be when James left Winterfloods.

MARY LYONS is happily married to an Essex farmer, has two children and lives in an old Victorian rectory. Life is peaceful—unlike her earlier years when she worked as a radio announcer, reviewed books and even ran for parliament in a London dockland area. She still loves a little excitement and combines romance with action and suspense in her books whenever possible.

Books by Mary Lyons

Don't miss any of our special offers. Write to us at the following address for information on our newest releases.

Harlequin Reader Service
901 Fuhrmann Blvd., P.O. Box 1397, Buffalo, NY 14240
Canadian address: P.O. Box 603,
Fort Erie, Ont. L2A 5X3

MARY LYONS

stranger at winterfloods

Harlequin Books

TORONTO • NEW YORK • LONDON
AMSTERDAM • PARIS • SYDNEY • HAMBURG
STOCKHOLM • ATHENS • TOKYO • MILAN

TO JACQUI . . . for many reasons,
but mostly for all the laughs
we've had together.

Harlequin Presents first edition February 1989
ISBN 0-373-11144-4

Original hardcover edition published in 1988
by Mills & Boon Limited

CHAPTER ONE

THE man slowly opened his eyelids, blinking rapidly until his eyes grew accustomed to the shafts of brilliant sunlight streaming into the room through the open casement windows. Lying still for a moment, his gaze wandered over the pale, honey-coloured, wooden panelling which seemed to cover the walls from floor to ceiling, the large stone fireplace whose grate was filled with a bowl of blue, white and pink flowers, the gateleg table covered with books, and the tiny, diamond-shaped window-panes set in gun-metal-grey lead strips within their oak frames.

Well, this hotel certainly seemed to be a step up from the usual anonymous, impersonal rooms that hotel managements throughout the world provided for their guests—he was even lying in a four-poster bed, for heaven's sake! Marty Goldman had really done him proud this time, and it definitely made a nice change from that fleapit of a hotel in Africa, where he and the rest of the crew had been dumped for the last month. Still, he couldn't lie here all day. Goodness knew what time it was, but it certainly looked as if he'd overslept more than somewhat. That damn jet-lag was a real killer, he told himself, frowning as he tried to lift his arm to check his wristwatch. The frown on his brow deepened as he stared at his bare arm. No watch? And why in the hell did the simple physical action of raising his arm seem to require such a strenuous effort on his part?

'This is damned ridiculous!' he muttered, trying to sit up and falling back exhausted against the pillows. Taking a deep breath before attempting to swing his legs out of bed, he was distracted by the loud sound of a cow mooing somewhere outside the room. Cows in London? Wow—that really was something else! He raised his head to look out of a low casement window opposite the bed, and his eyes widened with shock as he viewed the sight of lush green meadows rolling away to far distant hills. This wasn't London! *So, where in the hell was he?*

Stunned by the discovery that he obviously wasn't in the bedroom of his London hotel, he lay back on the soft feather mattress. God knew what was going on—he felt as weak as a kitten and his body seemed to ache all over, just as if it had been put through a grinding machine. It was no good. Try as he might, he simply couldn't seem to come up with any answers to the many worrying questions hammering away in his brain; and with a tired, weary sigh he gave up the unequal struggle, slowly drifting into a deep, dreamless sleep.

'Well, you've really gone and done it this time, Miss Polly, and no mistake!'

'Oh, come on, Elsie . . .'

'Don't you try and wheedle me, my girl!' the older woman retorted, banging a plate of fried eggs and bacon down on the table in front of Polly. 'Just because you've been down to London, and appeared on that there TV, there's no need for you to pick up all them Londoners' nasty, loose ways.'

'For goodness' sake!' Polly grinned. 'Listening to you, anyone would think London was as bad as

Sodom and Gomorrah! As far as I'm concerned, it's dead boring compared to what goes on in this village. You only have to listen to Mrs Jenkins at the corner shop to realise that Eastdale is riddled with vice and iniquity!'

'Them's disgusting words—you wants to wash your mouth out with soap and water!' Elsie retorted grimly. 'And don't you be changing the subject, neither. Fancy you bringing home a strange man, like what you've done... Well, I'm lost for words—and that's a fact!'

'The day you're lost for words, Elsie, will be the day that the moon turns into green cheese!' She smiled affectionately at the elderly woman, who had looked after Polly's stepmother, Alicia, when she was a child, and had subsequently stayed on at Winterfloods Farm as a housekeeper. Following her stepmother's marriage over five years ago to Giles Ratcliffe, the local squire who lived half a mile away at Eastdale Hall, Elsie had remained at the farm to look after Polly, taking a motherly and very proprietorial interest in the girl's affairs.

Almost too much of an interest at times, Polly thought, and this was definitely one of the days when she could have done without Elsie's care and concern for her welfare, however well meant.

'Don't you be so cheeky!' Elsie grumbled, banging the saucepans in the sink. 'And you is dang lucky your stepma and her husband is away in Australia, my girl. There's no way she'd approve of you having strange men sleeping in this house. As for what the Squire would say... Well, I don't need to tell you that Mr Ratcliffe is not one who is likely to mince his words!' she added, turning around to fix Polly with a knowing, beady eye.

'Oh, for heaven's sake! I'm twenty-six years of age, and perfectly capable of looking after myself.'

'Humph!'

Trying to ignore the housekeeper's snort of disapproval, Polly stared down at the fried egg on her plate. First Dr Martin, and now Elsie... She was sick and tired of being told that she'd been an idiot; especially since she was quite well aware that her action last night had turned out to be a particularly foolish one. But it was easy enough to see that now, in the cold light of day, she thought glumly. It had been a quite different matter last night when, tired and fed up with London—and the stupid man who had presented such a problem—it had seemed the only obvious, sensible decision for her to take.

She sighed and pushed a hand roughly through her curly red hair. 'All right, Elsie—I agree that I shouldn't have dragged that man up here,' she admitted. 'However, he's here now and we'll just have to make the best of it. OK?'

'Well—there's no reason for you to give shelter to all the waifs and strays you come across. You've quite enough to do running this farm.' The older woman glared at Polly. 'I well remember when your stepma first brought you up here, six years ago. You was a fine figure of a girl—and now look at you! The Good Lord knows I try to feed you up, but it's a dang waste of time. A girl your age has no right to be so thin and scraggy...'

'Thank you!'

'Well, it's nothing but the truth.'

'Oh, no, it's not,' Polly retorted. 'Far from having a ''fine figure'', as you call it, I was disgustingly fat. F-A-T!' she repeated, grimacing at the recollection of herself as a bored, plump twenty-year-old.

Born and bred in London, it was only after the death of her father, the industrialist and financier Sir Walter Preston, that she had accompanied her young, widowed stepmother to her family farm in the north-west of England. While her stepmother, Alicia, had promptly fallen in love and married Giles Ratcliffe, the local squire who owned most of the land in the village, Polly had proceeded to fall equally in love with Winterfloods Farm itself. Realising that she knew absolutely nothing about the science of farming, she had enrolled herself for three years hard, academic work at an agricultural college, after which—and thanks to the large fortune left to her by her father—she had persuaded Giles to sell her the freehold of the farm. It was a decision she had never regretted, and she took much pleasure in the knowledge that, for the past few years, she had made a considerable success of running a viable financial enterprise.

'If I'm now a lot slimmer than I was,' Polly added firmly, 'it's because good, healthy exercise about the farm has trimmed me down to the size I should have been in the first place.'

Elsie pursed her lips and folded her arms over her ample bosom. 'Say what you will, there's more to life than farming, my girl. What you needs is a man to keep you in order! You should be married and producing some children for me to look after, instead of spending your days fiddling around with those cows and that cheesemaking of yours. I'm not saying you're not doing well, because I know you are,' she added quickly as Polly opened her mouth to protest. 'But there's more important things than your precious "Shropshire Blue" cheese—that I do know! That nice young Dr Martin fancies you—and you could do a lot worse, I reckon. So what's wrong with him, a fine, up-standing man like that?'

'There's nothing wrong with him. I just don't want to marry him, that's all. So, please cross him off the list of suitors you keep dangling in front of my nose,' Polly said firmly.

'Well, I hope you aren't fancying your chances with that man upstairs, my girl! I had a quick look in at him earlier this morning, and I can tell you that he's far too handsome for his own good—and yours!' Elsie added grimly. 'I reckon you ought to pack him off to a nursing home, as quick as may be.'

Polly laughed as she poured herself some coffee. 'Don't be silly. He's obviously feeling too ill to be contemplating rape, or whatever nasty idea you've got tucked away in your horrid old mind!' She smiled over her cup at the small, round, squat figure of her housekeeper, who was surveying Polly with her ferocious little boot-button eyes.

'I didn't think any such thing!' Elsie's hard red cheeks flushed with indignation. 'But even if I did—and I'm not admitting it, mind you—the man's going to get better, isn't he? And then what, I'd like to know?'

'Then he'll go back to wherever he came from,' Polly said dismissively as she rose from the table.

'Dr Martin was very helpful last night. He also called in early this morning on the way to his surgery. Apparently our strange visitor has picked up some bug on his travels—and the doctor did say that he needs to be kept warm in bed, and given lots of liquid.'

'Humph...' Elsie turned to walk over to the sink where she began fiercely scouring some pots and pans.

Polly sighed and went over to put an arm around the housekeeper's shoulders. 'Come on, Elsie, don't be such an old misery! I don't know anything about the man, except that he's American and that he told the doctor his name is Mr Linklater. But you must see that, as he's obviously a stranger to this country, we haven't any choice but to look after him until he's better.'

'Well...'

'I knew you'd understand,' Polly said quickly. 'By the way,' she added, 'I've been meaning to ask about Mrs Renshaw's daughter? She must be expecting her baby any day now.'

'Oh—dang me! Didn't I tell you the latest news? Lily is expecting twins!'

'Wow—that will keep her busy!'

'I should say it will,' Elsie agreed with a fond smile. A widow, and not having any children of her own, Elsie had always had a very soft spot for her niece, Lily, the only child of Elsie's sister, who was housekeeper up at Eastdale Hall—as Polly had known full well when she had deliberately changed the subject.

'My sister is in a right tizzy,' Elsie continued. 'She wants to go and help look after Lily and the babies when they arrive, but she can't see her way to leaving the Hall empty. Not while your stepma and Mr Ratcliffe is away in Australia. Dead frightened of burglars breaking in, she is.'

'Well, if Mrs Renshaw feels she can't leave the Hall, why don't you take a few weeks off to help Lily?' Polly muttered, looking impatiently down at her watch. 'Oh, lord—look at the time! I must go and see Jim about the temperature in the cheese room.' Jim Moxon, her cheesemaker, was a fanatical perfectionist, and although it could be frustrating to deal with him at times, she knew she was lucky to employ someone with so much expertise. 'Besides which,' she added, 'the vet should be here any minute to see to one of the cows. So, can you be a love, and keep an eye on Mr Linklater? And make sure he gets enough to drink, won't you?'

'Yes, of course I will. But I still say it's not a proper arrangement—not for a young girl that's living on her own . . .' she called out as Polly made good her escape, disappearing through the door which led out into the farmyard.

Fully occupied with first the vet, and then inspecting the milk and cheese dairies, it wasn't until Polly got into her Land Rover and began driving down to the far meadow to see how the farmworkers were getting on with cutting the silage that she had any time to think about the events of last night.

If only she hadn't let herself be pressured into going to that dinner in London last night! Quite honestly, it now looked as if she had made a grave mistake, last February, in allowing those television people anywhere near the farm.

How could she have known that the result—*In the Bleak Midwinter*—a documentary record of her life on a snowbound, remote farm in Shropshire during lambing time—would have been such a smash hit with the general public? It simply had never occurred to her that the film might be nominated for an award, and that, as the 'star' of the production, she would be expected to attend the ceremony in person. If it had, she told herself grimly, remembering all the razzmatazz of last night's awards' ceremony, she certainly wouldn't have let the film crew in past the farm gate!

As it was, all the media 'hype' had left her completely cold. Not possessing a television set, Polly didn't know or recognise any of the famous stars of stage, screen and radio. She had suspected that she wouldn't have anything in common with the people seated at her table, and a few minutes of disjointed conversation with her fellow diners—who were far more interested in smiling into the many television cameras recording the event than talking to her—had confirmed her worst fears. The announcements and congratulatory speeches had been endless, seeming to drag on for ever. It wasn't until the producer of her film went up to the rostrum to receive his prize for the Best Documentary, and her corner of the large hotel dining-room was illuminated by brilliant spotlights, that her attention was drawn to a man sitting at the next table.

Polly had stared at the tall, broad-shouldered figure, rapidly coming to the conclusion that he was, without doubt, the most amazingly handsome man she had ever seen! And she clearly wasn't the only one to think so, her lips curving into a grin as she noticed the two beautiful, curvaceous blonde girls sitting on either side of him. Vying with each other to attract his attention, they didn't appear to be having much success, since the man lounging back in his seat was looking bored to death—and every bit as fed up with the proceedings as she was herself.

It was a moment or two before Polly realised that the man had turned his bronze, tanned face and sleepy blue eyes in her direction, catching her smiling, wry appreciation of the scene and responding with a shrug of dry amusement, before slowly lowering one eyelid—in what could only be described as a conspiratorial wink! Flushed with annoyance at being caught not minding her own business, she had turned quickly away to join the others in applauding the producer as he returned to their table.

Belatedly realising that her part of the award proceedings was over, and that she could at last slip away with a clear conscience, Polly failed to notice that the handsome man from the adjoining table was following her out of the room. It wasn't until she was standing outside the front of the hotel, and opening the door of her red Ferrari, that she felt her arm grasped by a large hand, and a deep American voice saying, 'So you decided to cut and run, too. Smart girl! How about giving me a lift back to my hotel?'

Thinking about the matter afterwards, Polly decided that she must have been startled and thrown off balance by the stranger's unexpected appearance. She certainly couldn't think of any other explanation for why she had so meekly agreed to do as he asked. And by the time she was beginning to pull herself together, and have second thoughts about the wisdom of her action, it was too late.

'It's a great car, I've got one at home in the States,' he murmured, settling himself into the passenger seat and adjusting it backwards to accommodate the length of his long, lean body. 'I'm sorry to hijack you like this, sweetheart, but I'm feeling jet-lagged and tired to death,' he added in a weary voice. 'So, be a pal and let's get this show on the road, hmm?'

The sheer speed with which events had overtaken her left Polly feeling flustered and indignant. The damn cheek of the man—springing up out of nowhere, and expecting her to act as a taxi service! However, it was no good trying to turf him out of the car now, and so, with a heavy sigh at her own folly, she switched on the engine and drew out into the street.

Although she had once lived in London, she found that she wasn't entirely certain of her way around Mayfair, and it took her some time to regain her bearings as she drove through the small side streets. By the time she found herself travelling up Park Lane, it suddenly occurred to her that she hadn't asked the strange man where he wanted to go. Pray God it wasn't somewhere miles out in the sticks!

'What's the name of your hotel?' she asked, taking her foot off the accelerator as she slowed down and moved into the nearside lane of traffic.

When he didn't reply, she gritted her teeth in annoyance. This was certainly *not* her idea of a joke, she decided, giving him a sharp dig with her elbow.

The only result of her action was a grunt from the tall figure sitting beside her, and she could feel a hot rush of anger flow through her body. If this man—whoever he was—thought she was going to put up with this sort of nonsense, he certainly had another think coming!

Making a quick and completely illegal U-turn, Polly drew up behind some cars waiting outside the Dorchester Hotel. 'This is where you get out—right this minute!' she snapped, turning to face him. 'I don't care if this isn't your hotel, it will just have to do. Because, as far as I'm concerned...' Her voice trailed slowly away as she peered closely at his face, noticing that his eyes were closed, his head lolling back on the headrest.

'Oh, no!' she wailed, giving him a fierce shake. 'I'm not letting you go to sleep on me! Hey—wake up. Come on, you... you foul man! Wake up—*at once!'*

Some moments later, Polly sat back in her seat, taking a deep breath as she tried to calm down and think about the position in which she now found herself. First of all, it seemed that there was nothing she could do to rouse her mysterious passenger, despite even resorting to slapping his face. Goodness—he really was quite fantastically good looking, she thought, as a shaft of light from the streetlamp illuminated the straight dark hair which was brushed casually off his wide brow, the square face with high cheekbones and a skin that was deeply tanned. She'd never seen a man with such long, dark, thickly fringed eyelashes, which gave a quite extraordinarily sensual appeal to his classically handsome features——

Clicking her teeth with annoyance at letting herself get carried away like a stupid teenager, Polly jerked her eyes away from the good-looking stranger, and stared out through the windscreen. What on earth was she to do with him? He had said he was dead tired—but maybe he was just dead drunk? However, although he hadn't said very much, his voice hadn't seemed at all slurred, and neither did he reek of alcohol. Why, oh, why hadn't she had the sense to ask him for the name of his hotel before he passed out?

'Oh, lord, how stupid can you get?' She swore briefly under her breath as she suddenly realised that he must have his name, and hopefully that of his hotel, in his wallet. Turning around, she felt inside the soft, grey suede jacket. No wallet? But there must be! No one went around without any money or identification—not in this day and age. Feverishly, she hunted through the inside and then through the outside pockets—finding absolutely nothing but a gold cigarette lighter, and a gold cigar case. Maybe his trouser pockets...? Her cheeks flushed as she looked down at the dark trousers, which seemed to fit his lean hips and thighs like a second skin. There certainly wasn't room for a wallet there! He was much too heavy for her to turn over, enabling her to examine his rear pockets—even if she could manage to do so within the narrow confines of the car, which she very much doubted.

Polly took a deep breath to try and stop herself from screaming with frustration. Here she was, stuck in her car with a strange man who was fast asleep; so dead to the world, in fact, that she couldn't wake him up. He carried no trace of

identification, she hadn't any idea at which of the
hundreds of hotels in London he might be staying,
and no way of finding out, either. And, quite apart
from the problems associated with the mysterious
American, there were her own affairs to consider.
She hadn't made any arrangements to stay the night
in London, and she also had the vet calling at the
farm first thing in the morning, to see to a cow who
was ill with mastitis. Staring glumly down at the
man who was still lying obstinately fast asleep in
the passenger seat, she came at last to a decision.

'I'm sorry about this,' she had told his unconscious form some time later as the red Ferrari
scorched its way up the motorway. 'You may not
want to spend the night in Shropshire, but I can't
think what else to do with you.' And she had con-
soled herself with the thought that she would be
able to put him on a train to London, early the next
morning.

And she would have done—if the damn man
hadn't been still unconscious by the time she'd
reached Winterfloods. Unconscious and ill, as Polly
had soon found when she'd tried to wake him.
Placing a hand on his forehead, she'd realised that
he was running a high temperature, and from his
disjointed muttering it had been clear that he was
also becoming delirious.

Rushing inside the house to the phone, she had
been relieved to find that Dr Ray Martin was still
on duty, and even more thankful when he had
agreed to come over to see to the man. Considering
that he had been called out in the middle of the
night, the young doctor's comments had been fairly
restrained.

'You're a total idiot, Polly! You'd better start praying that when this chap wakes up, he doesn't sue you for abduction and kidnapping!' he had said when she'd told him how and why she had brought the stranger back with her to the farm. 'OK, you take his feet, and for heaven's sake don't drop him!' he added as they began carrying the American's long, comatose figure through the hall and up the wide staircase to the spare bedroom. Banishing her downstairs to make him a strong cup of coffee, it hadn't been long before Ray had joined her in the warm kitchen, gratefully sipping the hot black coffee and wolfing down a large slice of one of Elsie's chocolate cakes.

'Mmm...that's great!' he said. 'There's no doubt that Elsie is a pearl beyond price, and her cakes are sheer ambrosia. I do wish you'd change your mind, and decide to marry me—and then I could have you *and* Elsie, too!'

Polly laughed. 'Honestly, Ray, you choose the damnedest times to propose marriage! We ought to be concentrating on the problem of that poor man lying upstairs. How is he, and what do I do with him? Did you manage to find any identification?'

'Cruelty—thy name is woman...!' Ray misquoted dramatically, before holding out his cup for some more coffee, and smoothly resuming his professional persona. 'The chap came to as I was examining him and, when I asked him his name, he announced that he was James O'Neil Linklater the Third—how American can you get?—and mentioned something about having just arrived here from Africa, before lapsing back into a semiconscious state. The name didn't ring any sort of bell, I'm afraid, although he does look vaguely familiar. Rather odd that—not carrying *anything* in his pockets,' the doctor added. 'One does wonder how the man got to the dinner. Maybe he had a girlfriend there, and put everything in her purse...?'

'Who cares how he got to the dinner!' Polly exclaimed. 'I want to know what's wrong with him, and is he going to be all right?'

'The good news is that your strange Mr Linklater is going to survive. He's a very healthy specimen— super-fit, in fact. I'll come by tomorrow morning—or this morning, I should say...' he added, glancing down at his watch. 'I think I'd better take a blood sample, just to be on the safe side. However, although he's running a temperature, he's already beginning to look a bit better. I'm rather inclined to think that what he has is some foreign bug—which he maybe caught in Africa— combined with a lack of sleep and the jet-lag you say he mentioned. He probably had a few drinks at the party, as well, which won't have helped. So, basically, I'd say he just needs plenty of rest and, when he wakes, to keep up the liquids as much as possible.'

Ray Martin was generally reckoned to be one of the best doctors locally, and Polly had faith in his judgement, although she hadn't slept too well last night for worrying that the American might wake, and become disturbed at finding himself in strange surroundings. However, her fears hadn't been realised, and when she'd looked in on him early this morning he'd still been fast asleep. As promised, Ray had come by at nine o'clock to take a blood sample. The prick of the needle had obviously disturbed the sick man, who had begun tossing restlessly about the bed. Commanding her to hold him firmly down against the pillows, Ray had continued his work as swiftly as he could, while she had pressed her hands down on the American's shoulders. Polly had succeeded in keeping him fairly still but, as Ray withdrew the needle and released the man's arm, she had quickly found herself clasped in a firm embrace, the stranger's arms closing about her slight figure like bands of steel.

'Don't just stand there! Get me out of this...this fix!' she had hissed, her face reddening with embarrassment as she'd found her breasts crushed hard against the stranger's bare chest, his warm lips pressed to her hot, flushed cheek. The faint, musky aroma of his cologne had filled her nostrils, and she'd felt momentarily almost dazed and breathless, before Ray helped to release her.

'Well, I'd say he was getting better, wouldn't you?' Ray had said drily. 'That looked like a very normal, red-blooded male response to me. In fact, if he can pick up your sex appeal in his unconscious state, I'm not sure which of you I should congratulate first!' he'd added sardonically.

'Stop talking nonsense,' she'd muttered, nervously tucking her sleeveless blouse back inside the waistband of her cotton skirt.

'There's nothing nonsensical about the fact that you're a very sexy woman.' Ray's eyes had swept appreciatively over her trim figure as he'd walked over to the door, adding as a final Parthian shot, 'But do try and keep your hands off the patient until he's better, there's a good girl!'

Polly had been furious with both Ray's unnecessary sarcasm, and his possessive attitude towards her. Putting out her tongue at his departing figure hadn't done more than momentarily relieve her feelings. And sitting here, now, watching the meadow being cut for silage, she was still simmering with indignation. Ray Martin had a damn cheek! OK, so he had been very helpful, especially in coming out at midnight to look at the sick American. But that didn't give him the right to imply that she was man-mad... 'Keep your hands off the patient,' indeed!

And Elsie was just as bad, Polly reminded herself as she reversed the Land Rover in the gateway to the field and drove back to the farmhouse. Only, as far as the old housekeeper was concerned, it was the other side of the coin: every youngish man who came near the farm was likely to be seen as drooling with lust! It was about time that everyone realised that she was perfectly capable of looking after herself.

'That man upstairs is awake at last,' Elsie announced as Polly walked into the kitchen. 'And he's not wearing a stitch of clothing!' she added in a shocked, accusing tone.

'For goodness' sake! I didn't undress him. Dr Martin must have taken his clothes off when he examined the man.'

'Humph!' the elderly woman gave a sniff. 'Well, I know all about the wiles of them Yankees—and so I told him,' she added, pursing her lips tightly together.

'Oh, lord—what on earth have you been saying?'

'Nothing but the truth—and that's a fact,' the housekeeper retorted. 'I well remember my mother's words during the last war. "Them Yankees," she said. "They be overpaid, over-sexed...*and over here!*" Dang right she was and all, as some of those flighty young girls in this village found out to their cost.'

Polly groaned. 'Oh, no!'

'Oh, yes—it was terrible what some of the girls would do for a pair of silk stockings!' Elsie confided in a hoarse whisper. 'You wouldn't hardly credit the goings on. The things I could tell you...'

'I don't want to hear any of that nonsense—and neither does the poor man upstairs,' Polly snapped as she strode across the kitchen towards the hall.

Hesitating outside the guestroom, she paused to collect her thoughts. Goodness knew how she was going to explain everything that had happened. She'd known that he was going to be considerably annoyed at finding himself miles away from London—but now, thanks to Elsie, the strange American was likely to be very cross indeed!

Taking a deep breath she knocked and entered the room. 'Good morning, er...Mr Linklater...?' she murmured, looking towards the figure lying on the four-poster bed.

'As far as I know, that *is* my name,' the stranger muttered, slowly raising his head. 'But since I'm rapidly coming to the conclusion that I seem to be in some strange, crazy place...maybe you'd be good enough to tell me just who you are—and what in the hell I'm doing here?'

CHAPTER TWO

PAUSING for a moment on the threshold, Polly straightened her shoulders and walked across the floor towards the man lying on the four-poster bed. Staring up at her through a pair of the brightest blue eyes she had ever seen, the handsome stranger, despite his obvious weak and debilitated condition, was projecting a physical aura of hard, forceful masculinity; the overriding impression of strength and resolution was emphasised by the determined set of his jaw.

'My name is Polly Preston,' she said at last, 'and you are at Winterfloods Farm, which is in Shropshire.' When he continued to gaze up at her with blank incomprehension, she added, 'If you were to look at a map, you'd see that we're approximately half-way up the west side of England, and about two hundred miles from London—if that's any help?'

He shook his head and gave a short bark of wry laughter. He'd often thought that the English were a mad race—and now he knew it to be true! Fancy trying to direct anyone around the States with that sort of crazy instruction: 'turn to the right at Washington, and then bear left at Cincinnati'! The little men in white coats would soon be along to carry you off to the local asylum!

However, as he looked closely at the girl, he had to admit that she seemed normal enough. And she must be, of course, the 'Miss Polly' referred to by that dreadful harridan who'd been in his room earlier. Although why the ancient old crone should have been so determined to protect this girl—who looked more than capable of looking after herself—he had no idea.

As she leant casually against the bedpost, dressed in a pair of tight jeans and a slim-fitting, sleeveless T-shirt, which made the most of the warm curves of her slender figure, he was aware of an air of cool, self-confident composure. Despite that mop of red curls over sparkling green eyes, and the cute, turned-up nose covered with freckles, there was definitely nothing of the 'little-girl-next-door' about this lady!

'I'd like to say that the information you've just given me is a great help in pinpointing where I am.' He gave her a weary smile. 'But if I'm honest, I'll have to admit that it's about as helpful and clear as mud! So, how about if we take it from the top, and you tell me what on earth I'm doing here, hmm?'

'Ah, yes...' Polly hesitated for a moment. 'The fact is...well, I suppose that I sort of kidnapped you. I know I shouldn't have done it, but at the time I couldn't think of anything else to do.'

Christ! He'd always known that kidnapping was one of the dangers he ran—but he sure as hell hadn't thought that it would ever happen to him! Now he came to think about it, no wonder he felt so weak and exhausted. They must have filled him full of dope, in order to try and keep him quiet... With an enormous effort of will, he forced himself to try and remain calm. He didn't have the strength to do anything about getting out of here, not just at the moment, anyway, and so his best bet was to keep this damn girl talking. That way, he might find out more about what was going on.

'OK—how much are you asking?' he grated.

'How much . . . ?' Polly frowned with bewilderment. Something seemed to be going very badly wrong with this conversation. She had expected him to be angry, both at finding himself miles away from his hotel in London, and at having been subjected to Elsie's maniac views about Americans. But it had never occurred to her that he would react with such overwhelming rage and fury. The blue eyes glaring at her were cold as ice, the body beneath the white cotton sheet tense as a coiled spring.

'The ransom, of course. How much are you asking?'

'Ransom?' Polly's eyes widened. 'Are you mad? Look, I know you've been ill, but I can assure you that I don't know what you're talking about!'

'You've just said that you'd kidnapped me . . .'

'Oh, for heaven's sake!' Polly laughed. 'That was . . . well, it was just a figure of speech, that's all. Of course I haven't *really* kidnapped you—what an extraordinary idea!'

He could feel the tension slowly draining away, quickly followed by an overwhelmingly euphoric feeling of relief. 'No kidnapping?'

'Of course not! Why on earth would anyone want to kidnap you, anyway?' she looked at him with curiosity.

'Oh, you know . . .' He shrugged his bare shoulders. 'It happens all the time where I come from.'

'Really? Well, I can promise you that, just as soon as you have regained your strength, you can go back to London—or wherever you like. OK?'

'I'll hold you to that!' he said with a grim smile, before relaxing back against the pillows. 'So, how about giving me chapter and verse on how I come to be here, "half-way up the west side of England"?'

Polly giggled. 'It was a bit of a mad description, wasn't it?'

'You can say that again! Hold hard a minute,' he added, as she opened her mouth to speak. 'Before you go any further, how about sitting down on the bed, hmm? I'm getting a hell of a crick in my neck, having to stare up at you like this.'

'Well...' She hesitated for a moment, suddenly aware of a most curious sensation as she stared down into those gleaming blue eyes. Giving herself a mental shake, she moved over to sit down on the bed beside him, almost glad to rest her legs, which felt unaccountably weak and shaky. 'All right. Where shall I start?'

'Begin at the beginning—and go on to the end,' he said firmly.

'OK. We were both attending a dinner in London. Do you remember going to that?'

'Yes,' he nodded slowly. 'Although I chiefly recall feeling dead on my feet. I'd only flown in from Africa some hours before the shindig started. So what happened next?'

As she continued to relate the sequence of events which had led to his presence at the farm, his smile faded and he groaned aloud as Polly explained that it was his lack of any identification which had caused all the problems.

'Without that, and having no idea at which hotel you were staying, I couldn't decide what else to do except to bring you back here with me. I must confess that it wasn't a very sensible decision,' she gave him an apologetic smile. 'However, maybe it's just as well I did, because the doctor says you've got some bug, probably aggravated by jet-lag.'

'Oh, God—I'm sorry, Polly,' he said, taking hold of one of her hands. 'What happened was that I came off the aeroplane almost stupid with tiredness and fatigue. Marty met me, and...'

'Marty?'

'Marty Goldman, he's...' he hesitated. 'Well, let's just say that he's a business associate of mine. Anyway, he met me with a hired car, and dumped me at the Ritz for a few hours' sleep. He also offered to turn all my cash into English money, and so I handed him my wallet, which also happened to contain my passport. He said that as he had a few things to fix up he'd lay on a car to take me to the party, and that he'd see me later, back at the hotel, with the right sort of money.' He gave a heavy sigh. 'I sure am sorry I passed out, and wasn't able to tell you where I was staying. I guess I've been a bit of a problem.'

'No... no, not at all...' Polly muttered uneasily, suddenly realising that he was still firmly clasping her hand. It was quite ridiculous to be feeling so— well, so odd at the touch of his warm fingers, and the action of his thumb idly caressing the soft inner skin of her wrist. Every time he turned those bright blue eyes on her, she could feel the fine hairs at the back of her neck begin to prickle, and a nervous shiver run down her backbone. Oh, lord, maybe she was catching his bug...

'So, tell me about this place, Winterfloods Farm. I heard some cows mooing earlier, so I take it you and your family are real farmers?'

'Well, I am. I own and run the farm myself—with the help of some farmworkers, of course. I mainly concentrate on arable crops and milk production,' she explained. 'However, two years ago I built a modern cheese dairy, and so now the farm also produces a blue-veined cheese. It's rather like an English Stilton, but we call it "Shropshire Blue".'

He raised a dark eyebrow. 'I know all about liberated females, but isn't it a bit unusual for a girl to be running an outfit like this on her own?'

'No, not really—not nowadays. Besides,' she smiled, 'while this farm of four hundred and fifty acres is a fair-sized one by English standards, to someone used to the American prairies it must seem like peanuts!'

'I'd say that it sounds like a lot of hard work for a girl on her own,' he mused. 'So, how come you were at that dinner in London? Are you also involved in the entertainments industry?'

'Good heavens, no!' Polly laughed. 'It was...er...nothing very important,' she added quickly, deciding that she really didn't want to get into any long discussions about the television film. 'Would you like me to pour you a drink of orange?'

'Yes, sure,' he murmured, letting go of her hand as he struggled to sit up.

'Hang on, let me help you. I don't seem to be much use as a nurse,' she muttered a few moments later, her face flushed with the effort of helping to lift his large frame into an upright position. Not to mention the fact that she had felt extremely awkward and embarrassed at having to place her arms about his bare, hairy chest.

Stop being such an idiot! she told herself fiercely. It wasn't as if she hadn't seen plenty of men without their shirts. Practically the whole of the farm staff worked bare-chested in the fields at haymaking and harvest time. But none of them had been quite so...well, muscular and well developed. And she had certainly never before been conscious of a mad desire to run her fingers over tanned, silky skin...

'As nurses go, you're certainly an improvement on that crazy old woman who was in here earlier!' he gave a short bark of laughter. 'She sure didn't like the idea of my being here—that's for certain!'

'Oh, you don't want to worry about Elsie. Her bark is far worse than her bite...' Polly swallowed nervously, her voice trailing away and her cheeks reddening as she tore her eyes away from his tanned body, the sheet having slipped down below his slim waist to reveal not only the hard, taut muscles of his stomach, but also the plain fact that he was lying stark naked beneath the light cotton cover.

She really *must* pull herself together! she thought wildly, turning to the bedside table, and lifting up the jug of orange juice. Of course he was lying in bed without anything on. Other than the clothes he had been wearing at the dinner in London, the poor man hadn't got anything else to wear, had he? It was a bit awkward, but she was going to have to find a way to broach the subject of his need for some clothing.

'So, who's Elsie? Does she live here at the farm with you?'

'No, she has her own cottage down the lane, but as she's been the cook and housekeeper here at Winterfloods since the year dot; she more or less regards it as her own home—oh, damn!' Polly clicked her teeth with annoyance as she saw that she had missed the glass, and poured some of the juice on to the table. She seemed to be going to pieces all of a sudden—what the hell was wrong with her?

'By the way, I'm sorry to say that—er—in all the hoo-ha of your arrival up here at the farm, I haven't given any thought to your clothes,' she said, handing him the glass of orange. 'What I actually mean is—um—pyjamas, and that sort of thing...' she explained, her cheeks reddening as he stared at her blankly. 'I ought to try and find you something to shave with, too, I suppose,' she added, noting the faint stubble on his chin.

'I guess so,' he said ruefully, lifting a hand to run it over his chin. 'However, there's no need to worry about pyjamas, because I never wear them.'

'Oh, really...?' Now what was she going to say? The thought of this man walking naked around the house wasn't just disturbing, it was...

'Hello! How's the patient?'

'Ray!' She turned, beaming with relief to see the doctor standing in the doorway, and going over to greet him so enthusiastically that he looked at her in some surprise. 'He—er—Mr Linklater seems to be much better—really, he does—and so I think I'll just—well, leave you both together...' Polly winced as she heard herself babbling such inanities, managing to summon up a brief smile for both the men before making good her escape from the room.

Entering the old farmhouse kitchen some minutes later, Polly found Elsie getting ready to return to her own cottage.

'I've got to leave early today, seeing as how I've got a man coming to see to my old washing machine. However, I've had a word with Dr Martin,' she added, fixing the young girl with a beady eye. 'He tells me that man upstairs isn't well enough to make a nuisance of himself. So I've made him a nice bowl of soup, and you just give me a ring if you wants me to come back and cook him some supper.'

'Thanks, Elsie, I was wondering what to give him for lunch.'

'Hmm. Well, I may have said I didn't like the idea of that American being here,' she mumbled, a flush of colour staining her cheeks as she walked towards the door. 'But, seeing as how he is sick...well, I hope and trust I know my Christian duty to them as what falls by the wayside!'

Polly grinned as the elderly woman shut the door firmly behind her departing figure, before realising that Ray would undoubtedly want his usual cup of coffee. Although why he should have returned so soon to the farm she couldn't imagine. Putting a kettle on the stove, she glanced down at the old-fashioned fender of polished brass from the inside of which, in a cardboard box covered with a soft blanket, came the soft cheepings of newly hatched chickens. 'And just make sure you keep your nasty sharp claws away from them!' she told the large black cat curled up on the old-fashioned rocking-chair, who merely gave her a glance of bland innocence before lowering his topaz eyes to concentrate on licking his paws.

She was just getting a cup and saucer out of the cupboard when Ray entered the kitchen.

'Well, I don't think you've got much to worry about, not as far as your unexpected guest is concerned,' he said cheerfully. 'He's going to need a few more days' rest, of course, but he appears to be recovering from whatever bug he caught with remarkable ease. I only wish I was as physically fit as he seems to be!' Ray smiled ruefully, patting his stomach. 'Maybe I should get in a few more games of squash each week—I felt positively flabby beside him.'

'What does he do for a living?' she asked.

Ray shrugged. 'I really don't know. I did ask him, but he only muttered something about "business interests", and as he was obviously not feeling too good I decided not to press the point.'

'Well, if he's as fit as you say, maybe he's some sort of athlete?'

'Hmm—a bit long in the tooth for that, I'd have thought. The chap must be about thirty-four, which is why I was so impressed by his condition. He's quite good-looking too, isn't he?' The casual query was belied by the keen, searching glance Ray cast in her direction.

Getting a milk bottle out of the fridge, Polly gave a dismissive shrug of her shoulders. 'I can't say I've particularly noticed his looks, one way or another,' she muttered, concentrating on pouring the liquid into a small jug. 'Would you like a cup of coffee? Or maybe a cool drink, since it's such a hot day?'

'No, thanks, I'm afraid I must dash. I only called in on my way to see a patient in the village.'

'What about Mr Linklater?' she asked as he picked up his bag and began moving towards the door.

'He was looking a bit tired when I left him, so just let him rest for a day or two, until he's got this bug out of his system, and then you can pack him off to wherever he came from. I don't suppose I'll need to see him again—unless the blood sample I took comes up with anything out of the way.' He glanced hurriedly down at his watch. 'I'm sorry, Polly, but I really must go. Give me a ring if there's no improvement in his condition in twenty-four hours, OK? 'Bye.'

Going back up the stairs some time later, Polly knocked on the door of the guestroom and walked in, putting a tray down on the gateleg table. 'Elsie has made you some fresh soup. Do you think you can manage to drink it?'

'I'm not feeling very hungry, but I'll give it a try,' the American said, levering himself up against the pillows as she placed the tray on his lap. 'Incidentally, I don't think I've thanked you for looking after me. Your doctor tells me that I wasn't in too good a shape last night. I'm really very grateful for all your help, Polly.'

'That's all right. I'm sorry that I had to drag you so far away from London, but Ray says that you'll be fit and back to normal in a day or two. In the meantime, is there anything else I can get you, Mr. Linklater?'

'I'm feeling a lot better already,' he assured her. 'However, there are one or two things. For instance, I'm feeling a bit out of touch, so could I have a look at a newspaper? And can we drop all this formal "Mr Linklater" business? My real friends usually call me James. Do you think you could possibly bring yourself to do the same?'

'I might just be able to manage that, James,' she grinned. 'However, there is a slight problem with your request for a newspaper. I'm afraid I don't have one. In fact, all I've got in the way of up-to-date news is this week's copy of the *Farmer and Stockbreeder*, and I don't think you'd find the articles about silage-making and calf-rearing very interesting!'

'No, I can't say I would,' he agreed. 'I don't know much about England, but I had no idea you were so cut off from civilisation up here in Shropshire.' He shook his head in amazement. 'Don't you even have a phone?'

'Of course I do!' Polly laughed. 'I think you've got hold of the wrong end of the stick. There are lots of daily papers available, it's just that I don't choose to have one. Just as I choose not to have a television set. I've got quite enough to do in the evenings without sitting for hours in front of the goggle-box,' she added, smiling at his look of surprise. 'If I want to know what's going on in the big, bad outside world, all I have to do is to switch on the radio, where I can get news bulletins every half-hour. As far as I'm concerned, I think we're all too hooked on the media nowadays, and a bit more peace and quiet in people's lives wouldn't be a bad thing.'

There was a long silence as James stared down at his bowl of soup. 'That's certainly an interesting point of view,' he said at last. 'A little eccentric, maybe, but definitely interesting! Tell me—do you have equally strong feelings about the theatre or—er—the movies, for instance?'

'Movies? Oh, you mean the cinema...no, I haven't been to see a film for ages,' she shrugged dismissively.

'Well, well...' he murmured, staring up at the canopy above his head.

'I don't think I'm at all eccentric, and I certainly don't live in a total cultural desert,' she protested. 'If I want to see a play, or visit any of the art galleries, then all I have to do is to get into the car and drive off to Birmingham, or down to London.'

'Hey, don't get me wrong,' he said quickly. 'I'm all for a life of peace and quiet, and as far as I'm concerned this place sounds just great. And, if you don't mind putting up with me for a few more days, that'll be fine by me.'

'Yes, well, I think that if you're going to be here for a while I'll have to see about getting hold of some clothes for you.'

'Clothes?' He looked across the room. 'I've got a pair of trousers and a shirt, so I don't think you need to bother.'

Polly blushed. 'Well, I was thinking more of pyjamas and a dressing-gown, actually. If you're going to be in bed for a few days, it might be—er—a good idea.'

He lifted a quizzical eyebrow. 'To spare Elsie's blushes?'

'Of course,' she retorted quickly, and then found her lips twitching in response to his cynical, mocking smile. 'OK,' she laughed. 'I'll admit that it's a case of my sensibilities, too. I'm probably a very unliberated woman, but I can't say that I'm used to men walking around my house stark naked!'

'Not even the worthy physician?' he murmured.

'Ray?' She looked at him in astonishment. 'Good lord, no! I mean—he's my doctor, for heaven's sake,' she added as he raised his dark eyebrows again. 'I don't know about America but, here in England, doing something like that would probably get him struck off the Medical Register.'

'That sounds a bit tough on the poor guy—especially since I got the distinct impression that you and he were more than just "good friends".'

'Oh, really?' she drawled coldly.

'Uh-huh.' His eyes gleamed amusement. 'I reckoned that was the reason why he was so anxious to tell me that I mustn't outstay my welcome.'

'Wow! You really fancy yourself, don't you?' Polly glared indignantly down into his handsome face. 'It seems to me that Ray Martin is not only being presumptuous, but that you, Mr Linklater, are clearly suffering from a swollen head!' she snapped.

'Oh, come on. I didn't mean . . .'

'You look tired. And, since you've finished your soup, it's clearly time you went back to sleep,' she continued in a crushing tone, picking up the tray and ignoring his protests as she swiftly left the room.

'Hey!' he called out, staring at the door which remained firmly closed. He sighed, his lips twisting into a wry grimace as he sighed and sank wearily back into the comfort of the soft pillows. No, she wasn't going to be returning to his room in a hurry. And he couldn't say he was surprised. He should have known better than to mess around with that particular lady! The combination of sparkling green eyes and those tumbling copper curls might be damn attractive, but he was surely old enough to realise that a man, if he possessed any sense at all, should treat redheaded women with kid gloves and extreme caution! Most of the ones he'd come across were an unstable, explosive mixture of emotions— far more dangerous than TNT!

God, but he was tired! He couldn't remember ever having felt this weak and exhausted before. However, he must try to phone Marty. And as soon as possible. Not that Marty was likely to get too upset at him not returning to the hotel—but if he didn't show up soon matters could get awkward. And, quite apart from anything else, it wouldn't be fair to upset 'Miss Polly', who seemed to be an attractive, amusing girl . . . until he'd tried to get smart—and then, pow! It had definitely been a mistake to try and find out her exact relationship with that doctor . . . His eyelids closed, their dark lashes casting a shadow against his cheekbones as he slowly fell asleep.

Polly stood staring down at the tray on the kitchen table, where she had banged it down in high dudgeon some minutes earlier. To have over-reacted to the American's casual remarks had been nothing more nor less than pathetic! And getting upset just because Ray had been exhibiting a hitherto un-known possessive streak was patently ridiculous.

She knew very well that it would only take one short, verbal swat from her to send the doctor swiftly back into his corner—and, in any case, why should she care what conclusions James Linklater had come to regarding her relationship with Ray?

By the time she had finished her own salad lunch and washed up the dishes, her usual good sense had reasserted itself. She was very seldom, if ever, ill, but on the few occasions when she had been confined to bed she had been bored to tears. It was obvious that the American had been similarly affected, having nothing else to do but indulge in idle speculation. After all, she had brought the man up to the farm, and now it was clearly up to her to make sure that he was as comfortable as possible. In fact, she told herself firmly, she was proving to be a rotten hostess. The very least she could have done was to have given him some books to read, for instance.

Feeling ashamed of herself, Polly went into the sitting-room and chose some volumes from the bookshelf. She hadn't any idea of James's interests, of course, but if she provided as wide a selection as possible he should find something with which to pass the time. Her arms full of books, she retraced her steps up the wide staircase, knocking gently on his door. Receiving no answer, she quietly lifted the latch and peered around the door.

So much for your good intentions, she told herself, regarding his sleeping figure with a rueful smile. Withdrawing as quietly as she could, she went into her own room, tossing the pile of books on to her bed before going over to open her cupboards. She'd be able to buy him some pyjamas and anything else he needed tomorrow, of course, but in the meantime he was going to need something to cover himself—if only for when he wanted to go to the bathroom. However, after a thorough search, all she could find was a long woollen dressing-gown.

Hanging it up on the outside of her wardrobe, she removed the jeans and T-shirt which she normally wore for the work around the farm, and went through into her bathroom to have a shower. Towelling herself dry, she paused for a moment, walking back into the bedroom to contemplate the garment which had been bought some years ago, when she had been very much plumper than she was now. Whether it would adequately cover the American's broad shoulders was problematical, but she had a distinct feeling that he wasn't going to be madly keen on the colour.

When James awoke some hours later, Polly discovered that she had been quite right—he wasn't.

'My God! You aren't seriously expecting me to wear that?' he exclaimed, his eyes widening with horror at the sight of the startling fuschia-pink dressing-gown.

'I know that it's not exactly ideal, but ...'

'Ideal? I should say it damn well isn't!' He gave a wry laugh. 'I may be feeling a whole lot better, but I regret to have to tell you that I wouldn't be seen dead in that thing—no way!'

Polly sighed. 'I thought you might say that, but what are you going to wear when you want to go to the bathroom, for instance?'

He laughed again. 'I don't know, sweetheart. However, if that's the best you can offer, I'll definitely guarantee to think of something!' He paused.

'Forgive me if I'm being too personal—but how on earth does a girl with such brilliant red hair come to choose a robe that particular colour?'

'Why ever not?' she said over her shoulder as she left the room, returning a few moments later to place a pile of books on his bedside table. 'Wait till you see me in bright scarlet—it's a knockout!'

'I bet it is!' murmured James. 'In fact, you're altogether quite a knockout, Polly,' he added appreciatively, his gaze sweeping over her slender figure, lingering on the wide belt clasping her slim waist, and the ripe fullness of her breasts, revealed by the scooped neckline of her pale lemon dress.

Busily engaged in pouring him a fresh glass of water from the jug on the table, it was a second or two before she registered the warm, intimate note in his voice. Turning her head, she saw that he had levered himself up against the pillows, and was regarding her with a disturbing gleam in his brilliant blue eyes. Suddenly breathless, Polly felt as if her heart had skipped a beat, the world dizzily turning on its axis for a moment before it slowly righted itself. She could feel the hot colour flooding her cheeks, reflecting the rising heat suddenly sweeping through her body, and it seemed to take an enormous effort of will before she was able to tear her eyes away from his intense gaze.

Striving for composure, she tried to concentrate on controlling her shaking hands, carefully replacing the jug on the table before edging away from the bed. 'Is there—er—anything else you'd like? Anything I can do to make you more comfortable?' she asked, amazed to hear such a breathless, hesitant note in her voice. She hardly knew this man, for heaven's sake, and yet he seemed to be having the most peculiar effect on her equilibrium.

'Well, now...' he paused, and then gave a heavy sigh. 'I don't know why, but I'm suddenly feeling extraordinarily tired and very weak.'

'But I thought you said you were feeling better?'

'I was—until a moment ago. I really do need a lot of sympathy,' he added mournfully. 'So why don't you come back over here, and give me the comfort of your cool hand on my fevered brow, hmm?'

There was a long silence as Polly eyed him warily, her doubts confirmed as she caught a fleeting glint of amusement in his eyes. 'Apart from being tempted to slam an ice-bag on your so-called fevered brow, I also have the distinct impression that you are trying to bamboozle me,' she retorted sternly.

'Perish the thought!' he shook his head despondently. 'You see before you nothing but a poor, sick man. One who has been inadvertently—and through no fault of his own, I might add—uprooted from his normal environment. Carried away by a strange female from all he holds most dear...'

'Oh, come on, James! You know why I had to do that. And I've already said that I'm sorry,' she protested.

'...only to find himself alone among strangers, grievously ill in mind and body, longing for succour. All he wants is some small crumb of comfort in his hour of need. Some human warmth before he finally passes away and is consigned to a cold, unmarked grave. And what does this hard-hearted woman offer him?' the American's voice rose plaintively. 'Nothing but *a damned ice-bag*!'

'OK, OK—I get the message!' Polly giggled. 'So, what do you really want? Within reason, of course,' she added quickly.

'Surely all is reason, when two hearts are beating as one!' he said in a throbbing tone, before spoiling the dramatic effect by rolling his eyes and giving her a wolfish grin.

'You're not sick—you're a raving lunatic!' she laughed, suddenly aware of feeling relaxed and ridiculously happy. 'By the way, I hope you never feel the urge to take up an acting career, because I can promise you that's the worst performance I've ever seen!'

An odd expression flickered briefly across his face. 'That bad, huh?'

'Pure boiled ham,' she retorted with a grin. 'Which reminds me—what would you like to eat for supper?'

'Polly—I don't like to complain, but I think we have a slight problem with this scenario.' His lips twitched with amusement. 'You aren't supposed to talk about food when I'm trying to flirt with you, all right?'

'Oh dear, James—I am sorry.' Her green eyes widened in mock dismay. 'If only I'd known...but I thought you were just suffering from a pain in your stomach!'

He laughed and held up his hands in surrender. 'OK, you win—game, set and match!'

'Well, I don't know about winning—but I'm still waiting to hear what you'd like to eat. If you can concentrate on such a prosaic subject as food, of course,' she added drily.

Giving a snort of laughter, he lay back on the pillows to consider the matter. 'Quite frankly, Polly, I'm not feeling too hungry at the moment. However, I'd like to make a phone call, just to let a friend of mind know where I am. And I'd also appreciate a long, cool, alcoholic drink.'

'I'm sure that you ought not to be drinking any alcohol at the moment.'

'I'm prepared to risk it,' he said firmly.

She looked at him doubtfully for a moment, and then shrugged her shoulders. 'Well, on your own head be it. As for the phone, there's an extension in my bedroom.' Polly hesitated for a moment. 'If you won't wear my old dressing-gown, I'd better go downstairs and get you that drink while you waltz naked along the corridor,' she smiled. 'My room is the second door on the right, and if you want to shave you'll find a small razor in the cupboard over the basin in my bathroom. Are you sure you can manage on your own?'

'No sweat,' he said confidently.

Deciding to give James enough time to shave and make his phone call, Polly deliberately took her time about mixing a weak gin and tonic, before slowly climbing back up the stairs. Reaching the landing, she found James sitting on a chair outside her room, with the lower half of his body swathed in a sheet.

'Are you all right? Did you manage to make your call?' she asked, placing the glass in his out-stretched hand.

'Yes, I got through with no trouble. As you can see, I decided a Roman toga was more my style than your day-glo-coloured dressing-gown.' He gave her a tired grin before raising the drink to his lips. 'Oh, God—that's wonderful,' he murmured, quickly draining the glass.

'I don't think you ought...'

'Honey, the reason I'm sitting here looking like Julius Caesar on a bad day, is that my damn legs keep buckling on me. I sure as hell needed something to help me get back into my bedroom.'

'You should have let me do the telephoning,' Polly scolded, looking at him with concern. His face seemed pale beneath his tan, and she hadn't noticed those lines of strain about his mouth before.

'I hate being this helpless—I feel such a damn fool!' he grated bitterly.

'You'll feel better tomorrow,' she said soothingly. 'Come on, I'll give you a hand.' As she helped him to his feet, she realised, for the first time, just how tall he was, finding herself staring up into blue eyes which seemed to be a good twelve inches above her own.

Despite James's obvious fatigue, a smile lurked at the corner of his mouth. 'Are you sure you're strong enough to take my weight?' he asked, placing an arm over her shoulder.

'Of course I am. And for goodness' sake stop moaning, and concentrate on staying upright!' she retorted brusquely, suddenly feeling disturbed and disoriented by their close proximity. Her pulse seemed to be almost racing out of control as she put her arms about his waist, her heart pounding at the contact of her face with his bare chest. The unaccustomed intimacy, and the feel of his warm skin against her cheek, was causing her to become sharply aware of hitherto unknown, latent feelings and sensations in her body which she hardly knew how to cope with.

James gave a snort of dry, sardonic laughter as she began helping him towards the bedroom. 'Tell me, Polly, are you always this bossy—or do I just bring out the worst in you?'

His harsh, mocking words brought a hot flush of colour to her face as she halted their progress to try and disentangle her feet from the sheet trailing on the ground. 'I didn't—I mean, I wasn't being bossy,' she muttered. 'I'm just worried that, if you fall down, I won't be able to get you back up on your feet again.'

He sighed. 'I'm sorry, sweetheart. I guess I'm a lousy patient, hmm?' He raised his hand to ruffle her curly hair. 'OK—let's try and get this show on the road.'

As they moved down the corridor and back into his bedroom, their progress became increasingly erratic. There seemed little that they could do to prevent themselves from stumbling over the large sheet, causing them to lurch drunkenly forwards as it wound itself about their legs and feet.

'I've been in some crazy situations in my time—but nothing like this, thank God!' he laughed.

Polly found herself giggling helplessly as they banged into the gateleg table and ricocheted off towards the four-poster bed. 'I don't think much of your toga! You should have swallowed your pride and worn my—*watch out!*' she yelled as he missed a step. Tripping over the sheet, he stumbled forwards, his action jerking her feet from beneath her. Falling backwards on to the hard, wooden floor, she frantically grabbed hold of the sheet wound around his figure, and a second later the heavy weight of his body fell crashing down on top of her.

CHAPTER THREE

'HEY—are you all right, Polly?'

It was some moments before the swirling mist in her brain gradually dissolved, to reveal the high cheekbones and tanned features of James's face, only a few inches from her own. Trying to clear her cloudy vision, she gazed up at him with dazed eyes, only slowly becoming aware of a heavy weight pinning her body to the floor. The floor? What on earth was she doing down here?

Striving to pull her scattered wits together, she realised that she was lying on the floor beside the four-poster bed, and it was James's body which was pinning her firmly down on the thin Persian carpet which covered the oak floorboards.

A deep tide of colour spread over her face. 'I—I don't understand. What's happened?' she croaked, trying to lift her hands to push him away. But she couldn't. The lower part of her arms seemed to be strapped to her sides as if she was imprisoned in a strait-jacket. 'I can't move!' she cried, struggling violently as she tried to free herself.

'Relax and calm down,' he said firmly. 'I'm not sure of what happened, but we seem to have got ourselves so tied up in this damn sheet that neither of us can move.' He looked down at her with concern. 'You obviously winded yourself when you fell. Have you hurt your head as well?'

'No, I don't think so...' she gasped, labouring to draw breath beneath the heavy weight of his body. 'We can't possibly be stuck like this. Surely you must be able to unwind yourself?'

'Nope,' he grimaced. 'I've got the use of one hand—but that's about it.'

'But—this is ridiculous!'

'I agree. But it doesn't alter the fact that we're stuck, unless and until we can work out a way to get ourselves out of this mess.'

'And how long is that going to take? You and your damn toga...' she groaned. 'If you'd worn my dressing-gown, none of this would have happened.'

'Oh, great! If you think I was going to prance around like a damn fairy in that thing, let me tell you that you are very much mistaken!'

'Don't be so stupid! Who cares what you look like? I certainly don't,' she retorted scornfully as she tried to wriggle away from beneath his heavy body.

'Well, I do,' he snapped.

Polly gritted her teeth in exasperation. 'I've never met such a vain, swollen-headed man in all my life! Here we are, in this farcical situation—and all you seem to care about is how you'd have looked in my gown. You must be out of your mind.'

'Out of my mind? Hah—that's a laugh!' he grated angrily. 'And what would you call a female, with hair the colour of carrots, who was crazy enough to buy and wear a robe that weird shade of pink, huh?'

'I'll give you *carrots*!' she hissed furiously, glaring up into his hard blue eyes. 'And get your miserable carcass off me—at once!'

'God preserve me from stupid women!' he exploded. 'What in the hell do you think I've been trying to do? I'm certainly not lying here for the good of my health!' he ground out with hard sarcasm.

Polly nearly choked on the hard lump which seemed to be stuck in her throat. She couldn't remember *ever* having felt quite so angry, both with the dreadful man who was keeping her crushed beneath his hard, firm body, and the overwhelming vexation of not being able to do a damn thing about it.

'I don't give a hoot about your health!' she snarled, drumming her heels on the floor with rage and frustration.

James gave a harsh laugh. 'Thanks a bunch, sweetheart. I'm really touched by your tender concern for my welfare.'

'I *was* concerned—and just look where it's got me!' she wailed, making a tremendous effort to wriggle out of the tight, constricting bonds which were keeping her a prisoner beneath him. All to no avail. 'Oh, God!' she panted breathlessly. 'I wish I'd never gone to that ghastly dinner in London.'

'That makes two of us, darling—believe me,' he retorted. 'And for heaven's sake, lie still. Not only are you just making matters worse but, if you keep on making those sexy, provocative movements, I can't guarantee to be responsible for my actions.'

A deep crimson flood darkened Polly's cheeks at the taunting mockery in his voice. How dared he make such an insinuation! He must know that sexual provocation was *absolutely* the very last thing on her mind. If only she could move her arms. She'd happily give every penny of her large fortune for an opportunity to slosh that cynical grin off his handsome, arrogant face.

'Worse? What could possibly be worse that this?' she exclaimed bitterly. 'And since you seem to think you know all the answers—why don't *you* do something? God knows, you've been nothing but a damn nuisance—and a pain in the neck!—ever since the first moment I laid eyes on you.'

A dangerous, icy brilliance glinted in the blue eyes staring fixedly down at her. 'Oh, yeah?' he growled.

'*Yeah!*' she lashed back, her temper by now well and truly out of control. 'Not content with grabbing me outside the hotel...'

'I did no such thing!'

'...you then barged and shoved your way into my car, demanding to be taken to your crummy hotel,' she raged. 'I've never known such disgusting bad manners!'

'*Bad manners?*' he roared. 'My God—now I've heard it all! Remember me? *I'm* the poor sucker who was kidnapped, and who found himself trapped in this benighted place, miles from anywhere. *I'm* the sick guy who's been insulted by some mad old crone straight out of *Macbeth*—and now *you* have the nerve to talk about bad manners? Oh, my...' he breathed with savage, terrifying menace. 'You have absolutely no idea of just how bad-mannered I can be!'

She gave a snort of derisive laughter. 'Hah! Nothing about you would surprise me, Mr Linklater. Absolutely nothing!'

'Oh, no?' he mocked in a dangerously soft voice, and Polly suddenly remembered—when it was far too late—that, while she was totally immobile, James still had the use of an arm. Even before she had fully divined his intentions, he had raised his hand from the floor to bury his fingers in her red curls, holding her head firmly as he slowly and deliberately lowered his mouth to possess hers.

There wasn't a thing Polly could do to stop him. She was helpless, completely at his mercy as his mouth crushed hers in a kiss of devastating intensity, forcing her lips apart to allow his tongue to conduct a ravaging exploration—a deliberate, punishing invasion of overwhelming sexual savagery.

An age seemed to pass before the hard, relentless pressure eased, and he at last raised his head to stare down at the girl trembling beneath him.

Stunned and totally bereft of speech, Polly quickly lowered her eyelids, but the image of his strained, taut features, the blue eyes almost as dazed as her own, seemed to be permanently etched on her brain. Through her shock and distress, she was aware of him swearing huskily beneath his breath, and the surprisingly soft touch of his fingers as they brushed aside the damp curls from her brow.

She gave a weak moan of protest as he lowered his head to gently kiss away the droplets of tears on her damp, spiky eyelashes, before his mouth moved to softly trace the outline of her trembling lips.

'Hush, sweetheart. Oh, Polly...I'm so sorry,' he breathed. The soothing, gentle touch of his lips moving over hers possessed a tranquillising, seductive quality that sent shivers coursing through her body, an increasingly heady warmth that she seemed powerless to resist. Almost unconsciously, her lips parted under the gentle yet insistent persuasion of his probing tongue, the deepening kiss firing her senses and unleashing strange emotions, quite extraordinary and hitherto unknown sensations that caused her limbs to ache and tremble beneath his hard form. It was if a stream of liquid fire was scorching through her veins, a swift tide of erotic pleasure that instinctively responded to the active stirring of his body where it held her own ruthlessly imprisoned against the floor. And then, somehow far too soon, she became aware that he was withdrawing from her.

'James?' She slowly opened her eyes, gazing blindly up at him as her breathless whisper seemed to echo loudly in the room. A moment later, she could feel her face burning with embarrassment. Oh, God—what on earth had come over her? First of all losing her temper with this man, and then... She quickly turned her head away, clamping her eyelids tightly shut as she tried to think what to do. What could she possibly say that wouldn't make the whole situation ten times worse? Her confused thoughts were rudely interrupted as she felt him throw himself sideways, and then she was sent rolling across the floor as the sheet was jerked away from her body. A moment later, she found herself being grasped by strong arms, which scooped her up as if she was practically weightless and placed her on the bed.

Lying dazed for a second or two, she turned her head to see James sitting on the bed beside her. Swallowing nervously, Polly's cheeks flamed as she realised that, not only was her skirt hitched up about her waist, but she had no rational explanation for that quite extraordinary—and utterly inexplicable—explosion of raw desire which had possessed her only moments before.

'No!' James said quickly, firmly grasping her arm as she tried to scramble away. 'Please give me a chance to apologise for my behaviour, hmm?'

As she hesitated, he relaxed his grip, brushing a hand roughly through his thick dark hair. 'I really don't...I mean, I've never...' He gave a heavy sigh. 'God, Polly, I'm so sorry. I can't even begin to think what came over me, just now. Sure, we were mad at each other, but that's no excuse for...for what happened.' He shook his head as if in total disbelief at his actions, leaning wearily back against the pillows and staring blindly up at the top of the four-poster bed.

'It—it wasn't your fault. Well, not entirely,' she muttered, her mind in a whirl as she tried to pull down her skirt. 'I'm afraid I...well, I lost my temper, and said a lot of things I really didn't mean.'

'You have absolutely no need to apologise,' said James in a tired voice. 'I'll make sure that I leave here first thing tomorrow morning. I'm just sorry that I should have abused your hospitality in this way, and...'

'No! I mean, of course there's no need for you to go. You're still not at all well. In fact, it was probably that drink—strong alcohol on top of an empty stomach was bound to make you...er...a bit delirious...' Polly swallowed nervously. She was making an absolute hash of this, and James must think her a complete idiot, but it suddenly seemed desperately important that he shouldn't leave Winterfloods just yet. After all, she told herself quickly, he still hadn't fully recovered from his African bug.

Swinging her legs off the bed, she walked over to look out of the window. 'I really think that we must both try and keep a sense of proportion, don't you?' she murmured, trying to control her shaking hands as she smoothed down her crumpled dress. 'What happened just now was merely the result of our mutual loss of temper, and I can see no reason why it should ever happen again. The really important thing,' she added, turning around to face him, 'is that I honestly don't think you are well enough to travel back down to London.'

'Well, I must admit I don't feel too good,' he said quietly. 'But if my being here is likely to make you feel uncomfortable in any way, then I'm quite willing to leave.'

She hesitated. He really was looking dreadfully pale. Goodness knew why she should be possessed by this sudden, urgent desire to keep him at the farm. However, she'd already made it quite obvious that she'd like him to stay—and she certainly had no intention of getting down on her knees and begging him to remain at Winterfloods. In fact, it was beginning to look as if she might be making a monumental fool of herself, and the sooner she ex-

tricated herself both from the situation, and this
room, the better.

'We seem to be going around in circles, don't
we?' she said coolly. 'I think I'd better leave the
decision to you. If you want to stay—that's fine by
me. However, if you would like to go back to
London, then all you have to do is to say so and
I'll arrange your transport. OK? Now, I must go
and see to various farm matters,' she added,
walking swiftly towards the door. 'I'll leave you to
think it over, and you can tell me what you've decided later.'

Escaping to her bedroom, Polly sank down on
the stool by her dressing-table. 'What is wrong with
you?' she muttered angrily, glaring accusingly at
her reflection in the mirror. Why was she getting
all flustered over that man? OK, so he was very
handsome—quite extraordinarily so, in fact. So
what? There were a lot of great-looking men in the
world, but that was no reason for her to be sitting
here shaking like a leaf!

Maybe Elsie was right, she thought grimly,
dragging her hairbrush fiercely through her thick
red curls. Maybe, by living in such isolation here
in the country, she was getting out of touch with
normal life? There were certainly no outstandingly
good-looking males around this neck of the woods.
In fact, Ray Martin was just about the only reason-
ably attractive young man that she knew. Maybe
she really was becoming a sex-starved spinster?

A moment later, she caught sight of her gloomy
expression, and was forced into a shaky laugh at
herself. Twenty-six wasn't old, for heaven's sake,
and she hadn't yet reached the point where she

looked hopefully under the bed each night! As for being sex-starved . . . Well, she'd had her moments in the past, but she'd never found anyone who'd 'made the earth move', as outlined in all the best romantic novels. Even Ray's kisses didn't produce even a slight increase in her pulse-rate, and had meant nothing more than a mild, pleasurable experience. So, how on earth was she to account for the earth-shattering, bone-melting excitement which had welled up inside her at the touch of James's lips?

Deciding that she must have been temporarily out of her mind, Polly made a firm resolve to put the whole unfortunate matter out of her mind. And when, later, over his cheese omelette, James told her that he thought he would like to stay on at the farm—'Just for a few days—till I feel a bit stronger.'—she was able to greet his decision with cool equanimity.

Polly leant over the wooden five-bar gate, sighing with pleasure as she looked out over the wide green pasture to where the river, deep and slow, wound its way between banks covered with pink briar roses and the tall spikes of purple loosestrife. Dusk was falling and the air was very still. The cows, idly chewing the long meadow grass, ignored the chattering noise of the rooks as they settled down for the night, and from somewhere in the distance the sound of church bells barely disturbed the quiet of the peaceful scene. It was, without doubt, her favourite time of the day. All work had ceased on the farm, and she was free to enjoy the peace of a walk through the paddock and the pastures beyond.

Smiling with contentment, Polly glanced at the man standing beside her. A lock of dark hair had fallen forwards, half hiding James's face as he gazed out over the meadow, absent-mindedly chewing a long stalk of grass. His thin cotton shirt was open at the neck, the sleeves rolled up above his tanned, muscular arms, his long legs enclosed in stone-washed denim jeans that hugged his hips like a second skin.

'It's easy to see why you're so crazy about this place,' James mused quietly. 'It reminds me of my childhood. Not that the farm is really like my old family home in Virginia, of course, but it seems to possess the same sense of peace and security that I remember—and which I haven't found anywhere else.'

'Mmm, it is lovely here.'

'So's the view from where I'm standing,' he murmured, gazing at her hair which had been turned to fiery brilliance by the last glowing rays of the dying sun. He reached out to briefly touch a stray curl with his fingers, before abruptly dropping his hand and turning away to stare at a passing black and white cow.

Polly frowned, throwing a glance through her eyelashes at his tall, rigid figure. The last two weeks, following James's decision to stay on at the farm, had been one of the happiest times of her life. They had become great friends, Polly being delighted to find herself so much at ease, and in such harmony with another human being. True to his promise, he had never tried to repeat or make any reference to that brief, passionate incident on the floor of his bedroom. And, as one hot, sunny day had followed another, she had almost managed to convince herself that the episode had never happened. But during the past few days there had been odd moments of constraint between them, occasions when, for no reason that she could see, he had become moody and withdrawn.

Although, to be honest, it wasn't only James who was feeling edgy and keyed up at times. For some inexplicable reason, she was finding it increasingly difficult to get a good night's rest. Despite the hard physical work on the farm, she found herself tossing and turning restlessly through the long, dark, seemingly endless hours before the arrival of dawn put an end to her misery. Her lack of sleep was obviously the reason why she sometimes felt so tense and strained—but that couldn't be the reason for James's dark moods, nor was it because he felt stuck here at the farm. He knew very well that he was free to leave Winterfloods at any time, and indeed she was surprised that he had stayed on as long as he had.

In the beginning, of course, it had been because of the bug he had picked up in Africa. And, although he had very quickly recovered from his illness, it did seem to have taken him a long time to fully regain his strength. However, he always reacted very strongly any time she suggested that he should have a check-up with Ray Martin. 'I'm fine,' he had insisted. 'It just takes time for these germs to work their way out of the system. Besides, it's years since I had the opportunity to let go and be totally relaxed—and I'm loving every minute of it!'

And he certainly did seem to have been enjoying himself. Rising late every morning, he would make his way downstairs and out into the grey-stone-walled garden, taking advantage of the unusually long hot summer to laze in the sun, or reading one of the pile of books she had placed in his bedroom. Seemingly content to amuse himself during the day, he would have a long, cool drink ready for her when she returned to the house at night, tired and thirsty from working on the farm. For Polly, the long summer evenings had been magical ones: walking with him about the farm in the gathering dusk, playing furious games of Monopoly or Scrabble, or enjoying a quiet contentment as they sat reading together out in the garden, when James would smoke one of his long, thin cheroots until they were driven inside the house by the fading light. Then she would curl up on the sofa and persuade him to relate more stories of his early life with his mother and father on their stud farm near Richmond, Virginia, where they bred racehorses; or listen to tales of his youthful adventures when, following his parents' death in a road crash when James was only sixteen, it appeared he had done just about everything—from crewing on a millionaire's yacht off the Florida coast to riding as a cowhand on the Kansas prairies.

Despite having obviously had a colourful past, he was strangely reticent about his present-day occupation. When she had asked him what he had been doing in Africa, for instance, James had airily dismissed the subject. 'Oh, nothing very exciting—just business.'

There was no reason why he should confide in her, of course. Nevertheless, now, as she looked at James's stiff, rigid figure staring so blindly at the scene before him, she found herself wishing that she knew more about the man who had so abruptly entered her world only a few short weeks ago, and yet who was also—paradoxically—someone she felt she had known all her life. In fact, James was definitely one of the easiest and most entertaining house guests she had ever known. He seemed to have no desire to leave Winterfloods, appearing to be perfectly content to spend the days in either the house or garden, and showing no interest in meeting any of the farm staff, her friends who lived nearby, or the occasional visitor to the house. Thinking that he might like a change of scene, she had suggested that they go out one night to a local restaurant, only to find that he hadn't the slightest interest in exploring the locality. But maybe he was getting bored, after all? Maybe that was why he was becoming so silent and unapproachable at times?

'Would you like to walk down to the river?' she asked quietly.

James turned, looking at her blankly before glancing around at the gathering dusk. 'I reckon it's getting a bit dark, don't you? Besides, I want to finish reading that book,' he added with a grin. 'I can't wait to find out what happens.'

'Oh—come on! Surely you know that all Russian novels end in gloom and doom?' Polly laughed, relieved that he had thrown off his momentary fit of gloom. 'I'm amazed that you've managed to stagger through *War and Peace*,' she said as they began to walk back to the farmhouse. 'I read it at school, and can remember falling madly in love with poor Prince Andrei.'

'That guy was a dead loss—a real wimp!'

'He wasn't!' she protested, leading the way into the kitchen. 'Don't you dare cast aspersions on my teenage hero—or I won't cook you any supper tonight.'

'Is that a threat, or a promise?' James teased.

'Oh, come on. My cooking isn't that bad.'

'Who are you kidding? It's terrible. If I hadn't taken over these last few days—we'd have died of malnutrition!'

'You may have a point there. This place isn't the same without Elsie,' she agreed, not having realised just how much she would miss the elderly housekeeper, who had left the farm some days ago to help her niece, and the twin baby girls who had been born unexpectedly early.

James grinned. 'I got kind of fond of the weird old girl before she left, and I reckon after a few more of your meals it will be a case of, "Come back Elsie, all is forgiven"!'

'Thank you!' Polly laughed. It had been some time before she had realised that, instead of the angry confrontations which she had been dreading, James and Elsie had got on surprisingly well. It had taken the elderly housekeeper a day or two to accept the fact of his presence but, by the time she had left to look after her niece, Elsie had become resigned to his continuing occupancy of the guest bedroom.

'I still don't approve of you having strange men in the house,' Elsie had said as she prepared to depart to help Lily and the twins. 'But him and me have had a word or two, and I've sorted out matters to my satisfaction. He's given me his word that he'll act as a gentleman should.'

'Oh, no!' Polly had given a deep groan, her face flaming with embarrassment. 'Why can't you mind your own business?'

'You is my business!' the elderly woman retorted sharply. 'Green as grass you are, and no mistake. Let me tell you that James has more charm in his little finger that I've got bones in my body, and it's dang unsafe for you young girls having gentlemen like him around—that I do know!'

'Well?'

She blinked, looking up at James in surprise. 'Well—what?'

'Cut out the daydreaming, Polly. I'm still waiting to hear if you want me to cook supper,' he drawled mockingly. 'Or are you planning to serve up your own version of ptomaine poisoning?'

'What cheek! However, I've no objections to a bit of role reversal, and you do look simply *divine* in an apron!'

'Watch it!' he growled. 'My *cuisine* may not be *haute*, but I'm *très, très* temperamental. *Comprenez?*'

She giggled. 'Well, I *"comprenez"* that your cooking has to be better than your atrocious French accent! OK, OK—I wouldn't dream of arguing with the chef,' she added quickly as he advanced threateningly across the kitchen floor.

'So I should hope! And don't smile too soon, sweetheart,' he said, looking down at her with a mocking, evil grin. 'I've heard all about English roast beef and Yorkshire pudding—so I'm downing tools tomorrow and allowing you all the fun of cooking Sunday lunch!'

Polly shook her head, backing away from his tall figure. 'I only wish I could,' she murmured sorrowfully, her eyes dancing with amusement as she glanced sideways up at him through her dark lashes. 'Unfortunately, I've already decided that we're going to have a picnic up on Wenlock Edge.'

'Oh, yeah? And just when did you make that decision, hmm?' he demanded, continuing to move purposefully towards her.

'About five seconds ago!' she laughed. A moment later, she felt her spine coming into contact with the kitchen wall, the smile on her lips faltering as she gazed up at the man towering over her. Time seemed to hang suspended between them, the world shrinking to encompass only his still figure and the blue eyes staring so fixedly down into hers.

Standing motionless, her senses transfixed by the strange, gleaming, iridescent light in his eyes, she didn't attempt to move as he slowly raised his hands, giving only an involuntary shiver as his cool fingers cupped her face, before sliding through the red curls to hold her head firmly beneath him. As an inexplicable, devastating excitement began welling up inside her, she instantly recognised the mind- and body-shattering emotion—it was the same electrifying sensation which she had experienced only once before, and for which she now knew she had been subconsciously yearning during the past two weeks.

And then, as if in slow motion, his tall body leaned forwards to pin her to the wall. Through her thin cotton dress she could feel his heart pounding in unison with her own hectic pulse-beats, her nostrils filled with the fresh, masculine tang of his cologne. The strong hands tightened in her hair as his face came nearer—so close that she could see each separate hair of his thickly fringed eyelashes, and the faint flush beneath his smoothly tanned cheekbones—his wide mouth moving with infinite slowness towards her quivering lips.

A small, unconscious sigh of contentment escaped her as the firm warmth of his mouth lightly touched hers. Once again, his lips seemed to possess the same magical effect, arousing the same thrilling, unstable mixture of joy and elation that she had felt before in his arms.

'Sweet, lovely Polly!' he breathed thickly. 'God knows I've tried—but I can't seem to keep my hands off you any longer. I . . .'

The sharp, shrill ring of the telephone, which was fixed to the kitchen wall, cut across his words. Polly jumped, abruptly jerked from her mindless state of bliss, and back into harsh reality. 'Ignore it,' James murmured, but she had already put out a shaky hand and lifted the receiver from the wall.

'Hello? Is that you, Miss Polly? Hello?'

Oh, heavens—it was Elsie! 'Uh . . . yes . . . I . . .' Polly gulped nervously, trying to clear her dazed mind and concentrate on what the older woman was saying, while attempting to ignore the hard, firm body pinning her to the wall.

'Who is it?' James growled.

She put a trembling hand over the phone. 'It—it's Elsie,' she whispered.

'Tell the old witch to get lost!' he muttered impatiently.

'I can't!' Polly wailed. 'I can't even get a word in edgeways. She keeps jabbering on and on . . . something to do with watching a film about link chains on the TV. She must be nuts! She knows I haven't got a television set, and . . .'

She was just placing the receiver back to her ear, when it was quickly seized by James. 'I'll deal with it,' he said firmly. 'Hello, Elsie, what's the problem?' he asked, moving away from Polly's trembling figure, and turning his back to her as he leaned casually against the wall.

Momentarily paralysed, it was a second or two before Polly managed to pull her scattered wits together. And then, as she saw that James was still busily engaged on the phone, she quickly turned on her heels and fled from the kitchen; dashing upstairs to the sanctuary of her bedroom as fast as her trembling legs could carry her.

After quickly locking the door, she staggered over to a padded seat beneath the open mullioned window. Taking great gulps of the fresh night air, Polly desperately tried to control both the breathless state of her lungs, and the heavy sledge-hammer which seemed to be pounding away in her chest.

What a fool she had been! How blind not to have realised exactly why she'd been feeling so uptight lately: consumed by nervous tension during the day, and so restless and disturbed that she had been unable to sleep properly at night. From the moment that James's lips had touched hers, she'd immediately known what was wrong with her. It very much looked as if . . .

'Come on—just who do you think you're kidding?' she asked herself roughly, brushing her hands through her curls, and staring gloomily out at the gathering dusk. There were no 'ifs' about it! The plain, unvarnished truth was, alas, only too clear: *she'd fallen hook, line and sinker for James Linklater!*

Of course, it could be that she had been seized by some sort of mad infatuation which would, in time, burn itself out. But she had a horrid feeling that she wasn't going to be that lucky. Not having fallen truly in love with any of her boyfriends, she had no yardstick by which to measure the depths of her present feelings. However, she was absolutely certain that never, in all her twenty-six years, had she ever felt anything that came near to the fervid maelstrom of emotions she had experienced when in James's embrace. Even just thinking about it now, recalling the hard strength of his body pressed so tightly to her own, she felt quite sick and dizzy with longing.

And that, unfortunately, was the nub of the problem. She ought to be considering ways and means of extricating herself from such an awkward situation, but she seemed to have temporarily lost control of her mind. She was only conscious of the wild elation engendered by James's kiss, and an overwhelming desire to be clasped in his arms once again—as soon as possible! Jumping up from the windowseat, she began pacing agitatedly about the room, before sinking down on the stool by her dressing-table.

You have got to pull yourself together! she mouthed silently at her reflection in the mirror. Unfortunately, the face staring back at her didn't seem to be getting the message. The trembling lips beneath the hectically flushed cheeks, and the brilliant sparkle in the emerald green eyes, were ample evidence—if she needed it, which she most certainly didn't!—that her emotions appeared to be getting well out of control.

Polly's cheeks flamed. She ought to be ashamed of herself for lusting after a man like this. And she was...oh yes, she certainly was! But castigating herself for her folly didn't seem to be having the slightest effect on the emotional turmoil in her brain, or the extraordinary sensations whirling and churning around in her stomach. With the small part of her mind which was still functioning normally, she knew that it would be massively foolish to think of James in terms of anything other than that of brief friendship. Only two weeks ago he had been a complete stranger, and any day now he would be returning to his own world—an existence which was obviously many light years away from her way of life on a farm in rural Shropshire.

OK, so he'd kissed her twice—so what? It was no big deal, she told herself firmly. He was, after all, an incredibly handsome man, and for all she knew he was probably used to kissing girls all the time. Surely only an idiot would try and build a hearts and flowers romance on the basis of just two kisses?

It was some time before she managed to achieve some measure of calm. Since James had made no attempt to follow her—which only went to show that he'd been merely fooling around, didn't it?— she decided to have a long, hot soak in the bath while she thought what to do about the situation.

An hour later she was no nearer resolving her problem. Whichever way she looked at it, she was drawn to the inescapable conclusion that she would have to tell James to leave the farm, as soon as possible. She couldn't hope to continue their carefree friendship, not now that she'd realised that she had fallen in love with him; and she was damned if she was going to moon after a man who wasn't interested in her. It was going to be tough—of course it was—but it was the only solution, the only method of self-preservation that she could think of.

She stepped out of the bath and dressed herself, armed by the confident thought that she had made the right decision; although it was a confidence that began draining away as soon as she began trying to think of what she was going to say. 'It's been nice knowing you—goodbye,' was unnecessarily rude and abrupt. But, once she began going into some long, specious explanation of why she had to ask him to leave, she was sure to make a mess of it, especially as she was feeling far too sick and unhappy to even think of a good, or even half-way reasonable excuse for doing so.

When she eventually managed to force herself to go back downstairs, nervous and tense as a coiled spring, it was a considerable anticlimax to find that James was nowhere to be seen. Not feeling able to face any food, she trailed slowly back up the wide staircase, her eye caught by a narrow band of light at the base of the old oak door leading to the guest room.

Now was as good a time as any to get the whole beastly confrontation over and done with, she told herself grimly. Bracing her shoulders and taking a deep breath, Polly forced herself to climb the last few steps and walk briskly towards James's bedroom, before her shakily held resolution could crumble completely away.

CHAPTER FOUR

HER emotional self-preservation was at stake, Polly reminded herself, ruthlessly crushing an almost overwhelming impulse to put off the confrontation as she opened the door, and marched into James's bedroom. '*C-crumbs!* Oh, lord...I'm s-sorry...' she stuttered, her face flaming with embarrassment as she found herself staring at James's tall, naked figure. 'I...um...I should have knocked...I never thought...'

'That's all right, Polly. What can I do for you?' he said, clearly not at all put out by her unexpected appearance in his room as he calmly picked up a short white towel and draped it around his waist.

'Yes, well—um—this obviously isn't—er—the right time...I mean, I was just...' *Oh, dear God— I sound like an utter idiot!* Polly thought desperately, all her firm resolutions of a few minutes ago now whistling down the wind. Swallowing hard, she managed to give him a shaky smile and said, 'I think I'd better leave you to get dressed.'

Despite its large dimensions, it seemed a very small room as she turned, walking slowly and reluctantly towards the door on feet that felt as heavy as lead. As she put out a hand to the doorknob, she sensed rather than heard James moving silently towards her. For the space of a brief heartbeat they both paused, their still figures caught in a moment of time, before he put his hands on her shoulders and gently turned her to face him.

James gazed down at the glinting green eyes surrounded by a mop of red-gold curls and the high, firm breasts of her slim figure. Clothed in a short white skirt made from some silky material, and a matching sleeveless blouse, her limbs turned golden-brown by the long, hot summer, Polly was totally enchanting, and his senses were now adamantly refusing to respond to the tight rein he had put on them over the past two weeks.

It seemed like eternity as Polly stared up at his taut, unsmiling face, the lamplight casting shadows over his high cheekbones. She could read no message in the unwavering blue eyes staring down at her, nor in the strongly arched brows drawn together in a faint frown; only the fingers tightening convulsively on her shoulders betrayed his inner tension. As the silent seconds ticked away, the air seemed to become highly charged with sexual tension, her resistance melting away beneath the dark, dangerous current of attraction that flowed from the man regarding her with such intense concentration. Her throat seemed to be suddenly parched and dry, her body mesmerised by the warmth and proximity of his bare torso, the stern line of his wide, firm mouth.

'Polly?' he said at last, his voice sounding strangely hoarse and strained as he raised a hand to brush a curl from her forehead. 'You do realise...'

'Realise...?' she echoed weakly, aware of nothing else in the world but the touch of his hand on her skin, and the heady stream of nervous excitement flowing through her veins.

'Oh—to hell with it!' muttered James beneath his breath, his hands sliding down her arms as he pulled her towards him, his dark head descending to take possession of her lips. She gave a faint, inarticulate moan as the warm touch of his mouth unleashed a wild tide of sensations that obliterated all conscious thought. Once again, it seemed as if he was some sort of magician, his lips containing the same bewildering, bewitching enchantment she had experienced before in his arms. It was all so perfect—*so right!*

Except that now... now it was far, far more. His kiss, initially a gentle caress as he savoured the sweetness of her lips, was now becoming more demanding as he devoured the soft, moist inner darkness of her mouth. Clinging to his broad shoulders for support, Polly felt as if she was almost melting with ecstasy beneath the hands roaming slowly and erotically over her body. Her ardent response provoked a deep groan from his throat, and a moment later she felt herself being swept up in his arms. Striding swiftly across the room, he gently lowered her on to the bed, gazing at her with such a fiercely intense, aroused expression that she nearly fainted at the tide of sweet, hot desire flooding through her body. As he clasped her in his arms once more, the mouth moving over hers was now subtly different, embodying a powerful physical need that matched her own deep hunger.

Drowning, melting fathoms deep in pleasure, she arched her body against him, surrendering herself to the demanding possession of his kiss without restraint. She trembled as she felt the touch of his hand on her breast, the heat of his fingers burning though the thin silk of her blouse as he sensually caressed the soft curves of her body.

Slowly and reluctantly, James raised his head, his breathing fast and ragged as he looked down at the girl in his arms. Her cheeks were pale, her lips swollen and vulnerable beneath the slanting green eyes gazing blindly up at him, dazed and lost in a deep mist of passionate desire.

He huskily cleared his throat. 'We—er—we have to talk, Polly.'

'Must we?' she whispered, reaching up to wind her slim arms about his dark head.

James shut his eyes and took a deep, shuddering breath. 'God knows, you do things to me that I've only dreamed about,' he muttered. 'But, yes, we must,' he added more firmly, slowly removing her hands from his neck and helping her to sit up beside him. 'Time is fast running out on us, Polly, and we've got a lot of things to discuss. You must know how I feel about you...'

'No, I don't—not really,' she murmured.

'Oh, come on! You can't be that blind, surely?' he said roughly, gripping hold of her shoulders and holding her firmly away from him as he studied her face. 'Why do you think I've stayed so long here at the farm?' he demanded, giving her an impatient shake as she remained silent.

Dropping her gaze, Polly stared down at her hands as she desperately tried to control the rising excitement and euphoria flooding through her body. She, who had been so preoccupied with her own deep feelings, now found that she was having difficulty in comprehending the full import of what he was saying. Did he really mean...?

Cursing violently under his breath, he swung his feet off the bed and strode over to stare blindly out of the window at the moonlit garden. *'God-damnit!'* he ground out savagely. 'Can't you see that I'm in love with you?'

Staring at the back of James's taut, rigid figure, her eyes filled with the wonder of his vibrantly masculine body, Polly knew that never before had she experienced such a moment of pure, unadulterated ecstasy.

'And I do, too—love you, I mean!' she cried, giving him a broad, beaming smile of overwhelming happiness, and throwing her arms about him as he returned quickly to her side. 'Oh, James—why on earth didn't you say anything before?'

He gave a helpless shrug. 'For one thing, I was your guest here—and I wasn't sure how you really felt about me—and for another... well, I gave that shrewd old girl, Elsie, my word of honour that I wouldn't let things get out of hand. Of course, I'd fallen for you straight away...'

'Really?'

'Uh-huh. I can't remember having so many cold showers in all my born days!' he grinned at her as she bounced on the bed with excitement. 'But, as you know, there's a world of difference between finding someone physically attractive, and being in love.' He paused. 'I'm not at all sure about the rules of this sort of game, sweetheart. I only know that I haven't felt this way about anyone before.'

'Neither have I,' she confessed.

'So, there are a lot of things we have to discuss, and...'

While he was speaking, her fingertips began tracing a path through the dark, curly hair on his chest, her lips exploring the broad length of his shoulder-blade and savouring the salty tang of his male flesh; her senses were excited and inflamed by the knowledge of her own power, as she felt him quiver beneath her featherlight touch.

'Polly!' Ignoring his cautionary note of protest, she grew bolder, her fingers continuing to move softly through the fine hairs narrowing down to his waist, feeling his muscles tense as she drew imaginary patterns on his flat, hard stomach. 'For God's sake!' he muttered hoarsely. 'Don't do that—or I won't be responsible for my actions!'

But it was a warning she was powerless to heed. 'Please... please make love to me, James,' she whispered, helplessly trapped within the grip of an ancient, primeval force that was totally beyond her control. Feverish with the passionate desire she had striven so hard to deny, her body was now pulsating with a hunger and need that demanded satisfaction.

'My sweet, lovely Polly...' he groaned, the blood drumming in his head as he felt his self-control shattering beneath the soft caress of her fingers, and the driving urge of his own arousal. Rolling over to cover her body with his own, his mouth sought and found the yielding sweetness of her lips, his hands savouring the swelling curves of her thighs and breasts before swiftly undoing the buttons of her blouse. As she trembled with pleasure, a low moan broke from her throat as his lips left hers to trail slowly down her arched neck, frenzied shivers of excitement shaking her frame at his warm, silky touch on her burgeoning flesh, the moist heat of the lips pressed to the deep cleft between her breasts.

Locked in passion, she hardly noticed his swift removal of her clothes. There was no part of her that did not respond to him, no inch that didn't quiver beneath the electrifying effect engendered by his hands and mouth as they sensually caressed her pliant flesh. As the ever-increasing tension became almost more than she could bear, a deep groan broke from his throat as he quickly parted her thighs; his fiercely thrusting body led her through a wild, elemental storm of mounting excitement, pleasure exploding inside her in wave after convulsive wave, until she felt herself floating slowly back down to earth once again.

Afterwards, they lay quietly entwined together, her head cradled on his arm, his lips buried in her shining, tangled curls. Drowsily content, Polly recalled his remark about Elsie—who had clearly known more about their growing love for each other than they had themselves. It was just as well that the old housekeeper couldn't see her now! A bubble of lazy laughter rippled through her slim figure, the slight movement rousing James, who drew her closer to him and kissed her.

It was all he meant to do but, as his lips trailed down over her soft skin to taste the sweetness of her breasts, she heard him give a dry grunt of amusement. 'God knows what you do to me, sweetheart—but it seems I can't keep my hands off you!' he murmured, teasing her body with his fingertips in a tantalising, featherlight touch that left her breathless with desire.

'James!' she gasped helplessly a few moments later. 'I thought you said you wanted to talk?'

'No—not *just* at the moment,' he drawled mockingly, the ensuing long silence only disturbed by softly whispered endearments and her low moans of pleasure, as this time he made love to her with a gentler passion and more leisured delight, ravishing her senses until she was reduced to mindless ecstasy as he brought them both to the exquisite satisfaction of mutual fulfilment.

Slowly driving a tractor back from one of the far meadows, Polly quickly swerved to avoid a heavy log of wood lying in her path. She really must stop daydreaming like this! It must be love, she told herself, suspecting that the fatuous smile which seemed to be permanently printed on her face had already raised some eyebrows among the farmworkers. And, knowing the village, she hadn't the slightest doubt that the wicked old gossip, Mrs Jenkins, who kept the small grocery shop, was having a field day speculating about what she would undoubtedly call, 'them scandalous goings-on up at Winterfloods!'

Too bad! Polly thought rebelliously. It might have been a whirlwind romance, but she couldn't remember when she had last been so happy, and was quite unable to recall a time when she frankly didn't give a damn what happened on the farm. Her whole life had taken on a new dimension since last Sunday—and she didn't care who knew it!

During the last six days, it was as if she and James had dropped out of time. The long, hot days and the blissful, love-filled nights, had followed each other like a string of shimmering crystal beads on a thread of pure happiness. She was bemused with wonder that this man, who had been a complete stranger only a few short weeks ago, should now be so achingly familiar that she couldn't imagine a time when she hadn't known or loved him. Caressed into trembling pleasure, brought with passion and tenderness to the full knowledge of her own sensuality, it was as if she had never really known what it was to be fully alive.

They could hardly bear to be apart. June had drawn to a close and, with the work on the farm slowing down as they dried off the cows who were due to calve in September, she and James were able to spend more time with each other: strolling hand in hand through the meadows, or sitting out in the patio, the evening air heavy with the languorous scent of late-blooming roses. They talked very little, and mostly of nothing very important, both seemingly content to exist in a time dimension where yesterday, today and tomorrow merged together in a shining stream of love and contentment, without beginning and without end. And even the weather, it seemed, had conspired to foster their romance, as day after day the sun blazed down from a cloudless sky.

Driving into the farmyard, Polly was smiling happily as she ran into the house and through to the garden. Surprised not to find James, and realising that he must have gone out for a walk, she quickly made preparations for a simple supper and then went upstairs to change.

By the time she'd had a bath, and put on her prettiest dress, Polly was beginning to get anxious.

Dusk was falling, and surely James should have been back before now? Striving to curb her nervous apprehension, she wandered aimlessly around the old farmhouse. She never knew what prompted her to open the door of James's bedroom—but as soon as she saw the jeans and the shirt she had bought for him folded in such a neat, tidy pile on one of the chairs, and the long white envelope on the pillows above the blue bedcover, her heart immediately began pounding with fear and a sickening dread.

Even before her trembling hands tore open the envelope, Polly instinctively guessed the message it would contain. Sinking slowly down on to the bed, it was as if the very air was closing in upon her, thick and suffocating, as she read James's brief, final words of farewell. Her face white with shock, she remained stunned for some moments before the dreadful pain and agony began to invade her trembling body. Tears of anguish filled her eyes, spilling over and running down her pale cheeks, the sheet of paper fluttering from her shaking hands on to the floor as she threw herself down on the bed, her heartbroken sobs echoing in the deserted room.

Polly made her way slowly across the yard, quiet and deserted now that the farmworkers had gone home for their supper. Although the early evening had once been her favourite time of day, it was now the one she most dreaded. She'd always loved the old Elizabethan farmhouse, but the warmth of its old timbers held no pleasure for her lately, the empty rooms seeming to still echo with the happy laughter of the halcyon, idyllic time she had spent together with James. It was ten days since he had left Winterfloods, and there wasn't one minute of those days and nights when she hadn't been racked with misery and pain. It was the long, lonely evenings and the dark solitary nights which were especially hard to bear. So many times she had fallen into an exhausted sleep in the early hours of the morning, only to wake at dawn to find her cheeks still wet with tears.

She had hoped that burying herself in work would help to alleviate the torment, the intense longing for the warmth of his presence and the deep, aching need to feel the caress of his hands on her body. But it hadn't helped at all, and she had been so explosively bad-tempered with her farmworkers that she knew she was in jeopardy of alienating the affectionate respect, and the good working relationship with her employees, which she had built up over the last three years. And all for what? A few, brief weeks of total madness, in which she'd acted completely out of character and made an utter fool of herself? She couldn't imagine even the most dizzy blonde of her acquaintance being so stupid— and, if any of her girlfriends had ever confessed to such a crazy episode in their lives, she would have had no hesitation in thinking that they were certifiable idiots. After all, what else could you call someone who had behaved the way she had? Who had fallen so completely in love with a man about whom she knew next to nothing?

Sighing heavily, she walked slowly into the house and entered the kitchen. Opening the fridge, she gazed listlessly at its contents. There was no way she could possibly face any food at the moment—

even just the thought of it was enough to make her feel queasy. Maybe she'd feel better after a long soak in the bath? She sure as hell couldn't feel any worse, she thought grimly, mixing herself a stiff drink and carrying it upstairs with her into the bathroom.

Drinking alone in the evenings is definitely not a good idea, she told herself as she lay in the hot, scented water. Elsie would have a fit if she could see her tipping back the gin, and ... *Oh my God!* With a yelp of dismay, Polly sat up in the bath, the glass slipping from her trembling fingers as she suddenly remembered that her old housekeeper was due to return to the farm tomorrow. And then the fat was really going to be in the fire! She'd never been able to keep anything hidden from Elsie—and, if she wasn't very careful, it wouldn't take the older woman more than a few minutes to discover *exactly* what had been going on while she'd been away.

Leaping out of the bath, Polly slipped on a thin silk gown while she struggled to control the panic whizzing around in her brain. What on earth was she going to do—or say? It was bad enough trying to cope with the deep, searing humiliation, the ghastly shame and mortification of knowing that she'd made such a fool of herself over James, but there was no way—*absolutely no way*—that she could bear to put up with Elsie rubbing salt in the wound, saying, 'I told you so,' morning, noon and night.

'Calm down ... calm down!' she muttered as she paced restlessly up and down her bedroom. All she had to do was to try and think up a fresh version of events. Something that Elsie would believe, and which wasn't too far away from the truth—an essential point since, God knew, she'd always been a rotten liar. Her feverish thoughts were interrupted by the sound of a car drawing up outside the front door of the farmhouse.

Hoping that it wasn't Ray Martin—she'd refused a dinner date with him once already this week, and he hadn't taken it at all well—Polly went over to peer out of the window. A second later she gave a strangled cry as her legs gave way and she slumped down on to the windowseat. Her heart was pounding like a sledge-hammer, and she closed her eyes as the room seemed to revolve dizzily about her. *James?* Of course, it couldn't possibly be him. Oh, lord—she must be hallucinating—completely and utterly out of her mind!

Still, it had looked very like him . . . Peering cautiously out of the open window again, the blood drained from her face. As the large limousine drove away, she could see that it really was James standing there, dressed in a very smart dark suit and . . . *My God—he had a cheek!* If those three pieces of matching designer luggage were anything to go by, the two-faced rat was expecting to stay at Winterfloods for some time!

Rapidly recovering from her shock and almost choking with anger, she sprang back into the room. It was all she could do not to scream with rage. After the past ten miserably unhappy days, which she'd spent creeping around the house and farm, feeling sorry for herself—and how she could have been so pathetically feeble as to have been moaning over that damned man out there, she had no idea—

it was going to be a real pleasure to tell Mr-bloody-Linklater *just* what she thought of him!

'Hey, Polly. Are you there?'

At the sound of James's voice, she clenched her teeth. Oh, yes, she most certainly *was* here! Her lips curved into a grim smile as she contemplated some thoroughly vicious, but deliciously satisfying ideas—such as pushing him into the large dung heap in the farmyard! But that could wait. She must first make absolutely sure that...that *snake* wasn't given the opportunity to worm his way into the house. And, since James was far too tall and strong for her to cope with on her own, she could only think of one way of enforcing her determination to keep him out. It was totally illegal, of course, but what the hell...desperate times called for desperate measures!

Trembling with rage, she ignored the small, sane voice in her head which was urgently telling her not to be such a fool; tightening the belt of her robe, she ran swiftly and silently across the upper landing and down the stairs towards a small room at the rear of the house. Once inside, Polly quickly unlocked the heavy oak doors of a tall cupboard, hesitating for a moment before choosing the item most suitable for her purpose. She was tiptoeing back down the corridor when she realised, from the sound of firm footsteps in the kitchen, that her hastily conceived plan was beginning to go awry. *Oh, hell!* He must have got in through the back door.

'Ah, there you are, sweetheart. I was wondering where you'd got to,' James said as he opened the kitchen door and saw her standing in the hall.

'Oh—really?'

Barely registering the chilly note in her voice, James stood rooted to the floor, staring at Polly's slim, barefoot figure as she inched backwards to lean casually up against the oak panelling on the far wall. 'I...' He swallowed hard, unable to tear his eyes away from the thin, transparent silk wrap clinging so tightly to her damp and obviously naked body. God knew why she was standing with her hands clasped behind her back, but the entrancing view of her full breasts, their swollen rosy tips thrusting against the diaphanous material, was just about one of the most provocative and sexually arousing sights he'd ever seen!

'Why have you come back to Winterfloods?' she grated.

'Hmm?' James looked at her blankly for a moment.

Feeling suddenly weak and sick with nerves, and almost overcome by a completely insane urge to throw herself into his arms, Polly took a deep breath as she stared at the man lounging in the doorway. It was so damnably unfair! No one had any right to be so outrageously good-looking, she thought, desperately trying to ignore the throbbing knot of sexual tension in the pit of her stomach.

'What are you doing here? What do you want?' she demanded breathlessly.

'My sweet Polly, what a ridiculous question.' His broad shoulders shook with amusement. 'I want you, of course!'

'Unfortunately, I'm not on the menu tonight,' she snapped, trembling as she realised that, if she didn't quickly gain control of this situation, she was going to be in *deep* trouble. Try as she might, there seemed little she could do to check the hot excitement flaring through her treacherous body, her senses instinctively responding to the sexual magnetism of his warm, intimate smile.

James gave a low, sensual laugh that practically made her toes curl. 'Oh, sweetheart—that wonderful sense of humour of yours—it really slays me!'

'That's the general idea, *sweetheart*!' she grated, producing the long, heavy object which she had been hiding behind her back. 'Now—get the hell out of my house!'

James froze as he found himself staring down into the twin barrels of a large shotgun. *God Almighty! What on earth did the crazy girl think she was doing?* Her hands seemed to be rock-hard steady, but all the same... 'I hope you know how to handle that gun?' he murmured quietly.

'Oh, yes. I won our local Clay Pigeon Championship last year.'

'Well, that's a mercy,' he said, his taut figure visibly relaxing, while he quickly considered his next move. What did they always say? Keep the guy with the gun talking, until you can get hold of the weapon... But nobody had ever told him what to do about being held at gunpoint by an unpredictable, redhaired woman! 'Do I take it that gun is loaded?' he asked smoothly.

'What do you think?' she growled.

'Hmm...I figured it might be.' He gave her a lazy smile. 'That's one of the things I love about you. You sure aren't a girl to do anything by halves!'

She glared furiously at him. How dared he stand
there, leaning casually against the door as though
he hadn't a care in the world. 'Get out of my
house—right now!' she snarled through clenched
teeth.

'Hang on just a minute!' James raised his hands
in an ironic gesture of surrender. 'We're not playing
this scene properly. It's not your fault, but, if you
went to the movies regularly, at least you'd know
the form. I mean,' he shrugged his shoulders,
'what's the point of trying to play the part of Annie
Oakley, if you haven't even read the script?'

Despite knowing that, with the gun in her hands,
she held all the winning cards, Polly was slowly
coming to the uncomfortable realisation that
James—God rot his socks!—didn't seem to be
taking her seriously.

'Cool it!' he commanded as she raised the barrel.
'I'm trying to tell you how this scene is played in
all the best Westerns. So why don't you just shut
up and listen?' He paused, but as she remained
silent, manfully struggling to control her anger, he
continued with his explanation.

'OK. Now, just before he kills the bad guy, our
hero always goes through a long speech about why
a man's got to do what a man's got to do . . .'

'Oh, for God's sake!'

' . . . and he generally gets to say a few good lines,
such as, "You shouldn't have stole my horse, you
low-down varmint," or "You've had it, Jake, seeing
as how you're the dirty rat who burnt down my
house . . ." and so on.' He grinned. 'Of course,
someone like Clint Eastwood is clever enough to

play the part without actually saying anything, but I expect you get the idea, hmm?'

'What idea?' she snorted with fury. 'I've never heard such rubbish!'

His lips twisted into a grim, dangerous smile. And, despite his indolent pose and the elegant, expensive tailoring which clothed his powerful frame, she felt a sudden cold shiver of apprehension feather down her backbone.

'The point, you crazy girl, is that I'm waiting for your explanation for all this—er—drama?' he drawled, his voice heavy with menace.

'You know perfectly well!'

He sighed. 'I'm rapidly running out of patience with you, Polly. Why would I ask a question if I already knew the answer?'

'Well, you bloody well ought to know!' she burst out furiously. 'Pushing off without a word, and leaving me that snotty little note. "All good things must come to an end" and "deeply and personally committed to a contract..."' she quoted savagely. 'OK, I should have guessed that you're a married man, but why in the hell didn't you have the guts to tell me so, to my face?'

He looked at her in astonishment, and then burst into laughter. 'Oh, Polly—you're priceless! I *was* committed to a contract, but it's a *working* contract, you dope, not a marriage contract. I can give you my solemn word that I'm definitely not married to anyone, nor have I ever been. OK?'

'No, it's not OK,' she snapped angrily. 'Why did you push off without even saying goodbye? You didn't give a hoot in hell for my feelings—you bloody man! And now...you've got the brass nerve to turn up here again, and...'

'For God's sake! Stop waving that gun around,' he warned urgently.

'I'll do what I want in my own home!' she shouted, shaking with rage and fury. 'Don't think you can smarm your way back into this house, and my bed, you—you oily rat! By the time I'm finished with you, I... *No—go away!*' she gasped as he began walking determinedly towards her.

'You're going to give me that gun, and then we're going to have a good long talk,' he said firmly, taking the weapon from her shaking hands and putting it carefully down, before taking her tearful, trembling figure into his arms.

'I hate you!' she wailed against his chest, the comforting warmth of his hands through the thin silk gown as he gently stroked her back, only making her weep more than ever.

'No, you don't,' he murmured, leading her slowly back into the kitchen. 'Now, I'm going to make you a hot cup of tea, and then I'll "tell all" as they say in the best novels. All right?'

Still racked by sobs, Polly could only nod as she gratefully accepted the loan of his large, white handkerchief to staunch her flow of tears.

Later, when her storm of weeping had subsided and she had the warm comfort of two large cups of sweet tea inside her, Polly felt slightly more able to cope with life. 'I still don't know what you're d-doing here,' she sniffed. 'I thought—well, that note you left me seemed to say a very definite goodbye.'

James sighed, pushing a hand through his thick, dark hair. 'It's really very simple, but there seems to have been a serious breakdown in communication between us. The fact is, sweetheart, that when I arrived in England I'd already arranged with my business associate, Marty, that I'd take a few weeks off work. So, coming up here to the farm proved to be no problem. And then...well, I found myself falling madly in love with this crazy, red-headed lady farmer!' He raised her hand to his lips, gently kissing her fingertips.

'Oh, James...' She gave him a wobbly, watery smile which prompted him to pull her on to his lap, and clasp her securely in his arms.

'Everything was going along just fine, until ten days ago, when I got a phone call from Marty to say that I was urgently needed in Rome, and that he'd already despatched a limousine up here to collect me. In fact, I'd only just put down the phone when the vehicle arrived. I didn't know what the hell to do,' he sighed. 'You were down in one of the far meadows, there was no one in the farmyard to whom I could give a message, and so I only had time to scribble a brief note before getting into the car and being driven off back to London. I'm really sorry, sweetheart, that I didn't make myself clear,' he murmured, his hand sliding softly over her silk-clad body as she snuggled up against the warmth of his hard chest.

'Yes, I...' she hiccuped. 'I suppose I do see what happened.' She paused for a moment, before raising her head to gaze up at him. 'What were you doing in Rome? I've heard all about that *dolce vita*, you know.'

He gave a dry, sardonic laugh. 'Well, you may know all about it, but I certainly don't! I was working flat out so I could get back here to you.'

'But why didn't you phone me?' she demanded.

'I did. Constantly. But, not being able to speak the language, I couldn't seem to get anywhere. Believe me, if you want to try making an international call from Italy, the best advice I can give you is—don't! In the end, I gave up the hopeless struggle, deciding to get on with the work and then fly back to England as soon as possible. Any more questions?'

She shook her head, burying her face in his shoulder.

'So, do you think you could change your mind, and decide that you don't really hate me, after all?'

'Well...' she murmured, suddenly feeling extraordinarily shy, and unable to look him in the eye.

'OK let's go for broke.' Brushing away the soft tendrils of hair from her face, his hand moved softly down to cup her chin, raising her face towards him as his lips trailed a teasing path down over her delicate cheekbones, until they hovered tantalisingly over her mouth. 'Do you still love me?' he asked huskily.

'Oh, yes,' she whispered, winding her arms about his neck, and responding ardently and passionately to the invasive mastery of his deepening kiss. She gave a small groan of disappointment when he lifted his head and smiled down into her dazed eyes. 'It's been a *very* long ten days,' he murmured hoarsely, as he helped them both to stand up. 'And, as far as I'm concerned, it's definitely time that I took you to bed!'

Sweeping her up in his arms he carried her up the stairs and into his old room, placing her gently down on the bed. 'Now, don't move—I'll be right back,' he smiled, before running downstairs and returning a few moments later, not with some of his luggage as she had supposed, but a black leather briefcase. Putting it down on the round table, he snapped open the locks and took out a thickly folded piece of paper.

'Here...' he said, throwing it on to the bed beside her. 'You might like to read through that while I get undressed, since you're already well ahead of me in the nudity stakes. My God!' he laughed. 'When I first saw you in that transparent robe, I nearly made love to you there and then—although pulling that gun on me was definitely instrumental in temporarily cooling my ardour!'

'Oh, please—don't remind me,' she winced. 'I can't think what came over me. I promise you, I've never...'

'Hush, it's all over now. Hurry up and read that document. I'm anxious to get on with other—er—pressing business!'

'Yes, I can see you are,' she giggled, blushing as she tore her eyes away from his magnificently proportioned figure, and the clear evidence of his arousal. Trying to control the eager anticipation of her own trembling body, it was some moments before she could bring her concentration to bear on the large piece of thick, creamy-coloured paper, covered in a fine italic script.

'Well?' he demanded, coming over to sit down beside her.

'I'm not sure...it's difficult to read...' she murmured. 'There's something about the Archbishop of Canterbury. What on earth is this, James?'

'Keep reading,' he muttered, putting an arm about her waist and slowly slipping his other hand inside her robe to gently fondle her breast.

'I can't possibly read anything if you do that!' she moaned helplessly.

'Yes, you can,' he said huskily. 'Come on—hurry up!'

'I can't think why...' she sighed, trying to focus her glazed eyes on the document. 'Umm...where was I? "...Whereas James O'Neil Linklater, Bachelor, and Petronella Elizabeth Preston, Spinster..." How on earth did you find out my real name?' she looked at him in astonishment.

'For pity's sake, get on with it!' he groaned.

'OK, OK—don't nag! "...whereas ye have purposed to proceed..." blah, blah, "...to be solemnised with all the speed that may be..." Oh, James!' she squealed in excitement. 'It's a—it's a...'

'...a special marriage licence,' he said as he bent to bestow a lingering kiss on her softly parted lips. 'I know it's not the usual way to propose, my sweet Polly, but I hope to God you'll say yes, because it's taken a hell of a lot of effort to get hold of that bit of paper!'

'Darling James—how utterly, fantastically romantic!' she sighed happily.

He took hold of her hands, staring intently into her eyes. 'I know that we've had so little time together, my darling, but I am quite certain of one fact—that I love you with all my heart.' He paused for a moment and took a deep breath. 'So... will you marry me, Polly? Will you have the courage to take me, just as I am?' he asked, his voice thick and heavy with emotion.

'I certainly will!' she replied, falling back against the pillows and laughing for joy, and for the sheer ecstatic happiness that filled every fibre of her being. This precious moment was all and far, far more than she had ever secretly dared to hope for, and her voice shook unsteadily as she raised a trembling hand to gently touch his face.

'I love you, James,' she said softly. 'I don't think that I had any choice but to love you, from almost the first moment we met.'

'Oh, Polly...' he groaned, clasping her tightly in his arms, his kiss everything she had hungered for during the past wretchedly unhappy days. There was no other reality other than the soft, tender touch of his hands on her body as he removed her silk robe, his lips tracing its departure with lingering caresses; no past, only the present pounding of her heart beating in rapid concert with his own as she eagerly welcomed the powerful, thrusting passion and total possession of the man she loved so much.

Much later, lying entwined together and still enraptured by the pleasure they had shared, she felt James's body stir beside her.

'Sweetheart?' he murmured.

'Hmm...?'

'You wouldn't really have pulled the trigger of that gun, would you?'

'Well, I might...' she yawned sleepily, smiling in the darkness as she heard him swear softly under his breath '...but as I somehow forgot to put in any cartridges...'

'You wretch! You do realise that you nearly gave me a heart attack?' he protested, rolling over to trap her warm body beneath him. 'I know that you're definitely one very tough lady—but don't you ever, *ever* dare to do such a thing again.'

'Of course I won't. And don't you ever dare to push off without saying goodbye, either,' she retorted breathlessly as he gently trailed his lips down over her cheek. 'You...you never did tell me about your job. What do you do for a living?'

'I'll tell you all about it—tomorrow,' he said firmly, before his mouth covered hers, his hands gently caressing the soft, silky skin of her breasts and thighs until once more she became mindless with desire, her faint, sweet moans of delight provoking a deep, husky growl as James's love-making became more urgent and demanding, and their two bodies became one in a mounting tide of overwhelming passion.

CHAPTER FIVE

'You must be joking!' Polly exclaimed, gazing at James in open-mouthed astonishment and disbelief.

'No, I'm not joking,' he grinned at her over his cup of coffee.

'You really mean . . . ? You're seriously telling me that you—that you're *a film star*?'

'Umm . . . I'm afraid so.'

'Ye gods!'

'Come on, Polly. It's just a job—not the end of the world.' His blue eyes gleamed with amusement as she continued to stare at him in stunned amazement. 'After all, I might well be a mortician, with a syringe full of embalming fluid in my briefcase; or possibly a taxidermist, busily measuring up one of your cows; or . . .'

'Now you're being ridiculous!'

James shook his head. 'Not at all. They are also jobs or professions, just like mine. A little gruesome, maybe, but someone has to do them.'

'But . . . but . . .' She waved her hands distractedly in the air. 'You look so normal!'

'Gee, thanks.'

'You know what I mean.' She gave a helpless shrug. 'The whole idea of you being a film star is so extraordinary and outlandish that I just can't seem to credit it, somehow. Although . . .' she paused, putting her head on one side as she con-

sidered his handsome features, '... you are terribly
good-looking, of course...'

'Thanks again,' he murmured drily.

'Oh, shut up!'

James laughed. 'I wondered just how long it
would take my sweet, sexy, deliciously warm and
tender Petronella Preston, to revert back to being
the tough, bossy "Miss Polly" that I know and
love.' He glanced down at his watch. 'Do you realise that we've been happily engaged for almost
twelve hours, without one word of disagreement
between us? Wow—it must be a record!'

'Just watch it, ducky, or your new fiancée is likely
to hit you over the head with a rolling pin,' she
grinned. 'In fact, the only thing that's saved you
so far are all those lovely, flattering adjectives,' she
added, a faint flush staining her cheeks. 'Do—do
you really think I'm sexy?'

He looked at her, sorrowfully shaking his head
and clicking his teeth with obvious regret. 'Oh dear,
I wish you hadn't asked me that, Polly. But, well,
I guess you're the sort of girl who'd prefer to be
told the unvarnished truth, huh? The fact is,' he
gave a heavy sigh, 'I had a really terrible time last
night. How often did we make love?' He raised a
dark eyebrow, his eyes glinting with laughter. 'Believe me, it was sheer torture! I don't know how I
managed to force myself to...' He quickly ducked
his head as a piece of toast flew past his ear.

'You rotter!'

'Relax, sweetheart, you know I was only
kidding,' he said quickly as she reached forwards
to pick up the butter dish. 'I can't think why you
seem so unsure of your own attraction, but I'm

quite willing to give you a signed statement. How about, ''Polly Preston is the sexiest thing on two legs''?'

'As they say in those credit card advertisements—''That will do nicely''!' she giggled. 'However, I'd better warn you that your days are numbered if you ever call me Petronella again. And don't think I'm not going to put you through the third degree, and find out *exactly* how you got hold of that classified information,' she added grimly. 'However, I want to sort out this ''film star'' nonsense first of all.'

She took a bite from her slice of toast and marmalade, staring intently at James, who was leaning back in his chair, smoking one of his cheroots and regarding her with a wry, watchful expression on his face.

'My God—you really are telling the truth, aren't you?' she said slowly, trying to come to terms with the startling fact of James's profession. 'Are you very famous?'

'Well known is probably a better description. I used to be able to have a really nice, quiet time here in England, but now that they've been showing some of my old films on TV...' He shrugged his shoulders.

She frowned. 'I haven't got a television set, of course, but if you're that well known, shouldn't I at least have heard of you?'

'Ah...well, sweetheart, the fact is that I don't act under my own name. Professionally speaking, I'm known as Link Jameson. It was my first agent's idea,' he explained as she looked at him in bafflement. 'He felt my own name didn't have enough pazazz, or whatever, and so he suggested taking "Link" from Linklater, and tacking on the first two letters of O'Neil to James—making "Jameson".'

'It all sounds terribly complicated and confusing. And, although I'm sure that I've never seen you in the cinema, your name does seem vaguely familiar somehow...' murmured Polly, frowning and biting her lip as she tried to think where she'd heard his name before.

'I know the answer to that question!' James gave a rueful laugh. 'My God—I nearly died when Elsie rang here after seeing one of my films on TV. Luckily, the old girl was so surprised that she wasn't making much sense and I managed to get the phone away from you in the nick of time,' he grinned. 'But it was a damn near thing!'

Polly glowered at him. 'Are you trying to tell me that Elsie has known all along about you? And about us?' she demanded angrily. 'Well, of all the...'

'Hold it, sweetheart!' he said firmly. 'Once Elsie had found out who I was, she wasn't likely to keep silent, was she? So I didn't see that I had any alternative but to explain my serious intentions as far as you were concerned.'

'But I didn't know anything about your so-called "serious intentions". I...well, I wasn't even sure how I felt about you at that point,' Polly complained.

'And that's precisely what I told Elsie, begging her not to say anything until I'd sorted matters out between us. I knew I was on a very tight schedule, and I was terrified that the whole affair would blow up in my face,' he sighed. 'I had to find out whether you felt as much for me as I hoped you did, and then arrange for us to be married as soon as possible, since I have to start work on a new movie in a few weeks' time. Believe me, I needed that trip to Rome to do a "voice-over" like I needed a hole in the head!'

'But why didn't you tell me who you were straight away?'

James leaned back in his chair. 'Just look at how you reacted when I told you my true identity—a real case of shock, horror and dismay!' He gave her a bleak smile. 'Although, to be fair, that sort of response is a trifle unusual. On the whole, and however immodest it may sound, women generally become a real headache, "ooing and aahing" all over the place. And most of the guys in the street can't seem to see that I'm an equally ordinary guy, who's just doing a job that isn't half as glamorous as it's supposed to be.'

With a heavy sigh, James pushed a hand roughly through his dark hair. 'I'm not knocking the movie business; I've had a good life and I've made an awful lot of money. However, most of the time it's damn hard work, and you're only as good as your last film. You wouldn't believe just how easily today's star can become tomorrow's has-been,' he said ruefully. 'And none of us is under any illusions that, along with the stardom and the financial rewards, we also have to accept a total lack of privacy.'

Polly looked at him with concern. 'I've never really thought about it before. You must hate all the fuss—I know I would.'

'To tell you the truth, sweetheart, I've got so used to it by now that it doesn't bother me too much. But I don't know why you seem so surprised about the penalties of fame. Surely, with that TV film about your farm, you ought to be used to it by now?'

'How on earth did you find out about that?'

He laughed at the blank astonishment on her face. 'Marty's wife was over the moon about some programme she'd seen, and kept nagging him to watch the video. So, when I gave him instructions to get hold of the birth certificates, and all the other paperwork necessary for our marriage licence, he recognised your name and quickly put two and two together.'

Polly stared down at the table, absent-mindedly stirring a spoon around in her cup of coffee. 'Have you . . . no, I don't suppose . . .'

'Have I seen it? Of course I have—Marty gave me a video copy to take with me to Rome. I thought it was really great, darling, and I'm very proud of you,' he added with a warm smile. 'I don't know why you never told me about it, but I guess you value anonymity as much as I do, huh?'

'Well, to be truthful, James, I honestly don't think I'm cut out for fame and fortune.' She shrugged her shoulders. 'I really hated all the publicity—and the sooner everyone forgets all about that damn film, the happier I'll be!'

He frowned. 'It wasn't that bad, surely?'

'Oh, yes it was! I simply loathed every minute of the razzmatazz.'

'Hmm . . .' James looked at her blankly for a moment, as though he was doing complicated sums in his head. 'I hadn't realised that you felt so strongly about that sort of media attention,' he said at last. 'We could have a real problem there, sweetheart. Of course, I'd try and protect you as much as possible, but it won't be easy.'

'Oh, I can't see any problem,' said Polly blithely. 'It's you the Press are interested in, not me. Although, thanks to my own experience, I do understand how awful it must be to be recognised everywhere you go.'

He smiled and shrugged his shoulders. 'I think we're agreed it isn't exactly a picnic. That's why those weeks I spent up here at the farm, without anyone having any idea of my real identity, were just about one of the best times of my life.'

'I'm glad to hear that!' She gave him a shaky smile. 'Because I was just beginning to wonder whether you hadn't been bored out of your mind...'

'Absolutely not!' he said emphatically. 'Quite apart from our personal relationship, Winterfloods itself has become a very important part of my life. Neither you nor anyone here knew anything about me, and you accepted me just as I am. As far as I'm concerned, this place is a haven of peace and quiet—something I don't get too much of, I'm afraid.'

'Are you sure you don't mind that I ... well, that I don't seem to know a famous film star when I see one?' she asked. If he really was as well known as he said, James must have thought her quite idiotic and a total fool for not having recognised him immediately.

He got to his feet and came around to the other side of the table, pulling Polly to her feet and into his arms.

'I know what you're thinking, and you can stop it—right now,' he said firmly, staring down into her green eyes. 'I want you to understand, and always remember, that it's very important to me that you *didn't* know who I was. You, my sweet Polly, took me into your home and into your heart, simply because you wanted to—and for no other ulterior motive. You weren't interested in my celebrity status, or my money, or any of the hundred and one reasons why people are drawn to those they consider public figures.' He gave her a broad smile. 'You didn't give a damn who I was or wasn't—and I loved it!'

'Is that why...? Is it because I didn't know who you were...are...that you want to marry me?'

James swore briefly under his breath. 'There are times, sweetheart, when you really are an idiot! And I wish I knew why such a basically cool, strong girl should be so unsure of herself emotionally.' He sighed and gave her a slight shake of the shoulders. 'There are so many reasons why I love you, it would take me just about all day to go through them. But I can give you a few items, such as—you're damn funny and you make me laugh, you seem very tough on the surface, but you're really soft candy underneath, I'm crazy about redheads, and I find you so damn attractive that I can't seem to keep my hands off your lovely, sweet body. Will those do to go on with?'

'Hmm...I think so—to go on with,' she teased, smiling happily up at him.

'I think that I might have forgotten to mention one of the most important items,' he murmured, his arms tightening about her slim figure. 'I need you to love me as I love you, Polly,' he added huskily. 'Without you ... without the warmth and tenderness of your love, I know that my life will be nothing but an empty, barren wilderness.'

'Oh, darling ...' she whispered, gently pressing her lips to his cheek and feeling the quiver that ran through his body, his mouth searching for and then covering hers with an urgency that made her feel faint and dizzy. There seemed to be large kettle-drums pounding away in her head, her fingers clenching in his thick dark hair as she trembled helplessly against him.

'I think it's definitely bedtime!' he whispered, quickly sweeping her up in his arms and kicking open the kitchen door, before walking swiftly towards the wide staircase.

'*James!* We can't ... we've only just had breakfast!'

'Oh, yes, we can!' he laughed, tossing her down on to the bed, where she lay winded for a moment, staring at him with dazed eyes as he quickly stripped off his clothes. 'Besides, I haven't made love to you for at least two whole hours,' he muttered urgently, swiftly unbuttoning her blouse and sliding the jeans down over her trembling legs, carelessly tossing aside the rest of her flimsy underwear to run his hands over her naked, quivering body. The rising desire engendered by the sensual, intimate touch of his fingers clouded her mind, and she rapidly lost all sense of time and place, spinning helplessly in a whirlpool of sensual pleasure as James merged his own body with hers; drowning in the final agonising delight of a rhythmic, pulsating climax that caused her to cry out with overwhelming joy and ecstasy.

Later in the day, as they wandered hand in hand down the small lane towards the river, Polly realised she had so many questions to ask James that she really didn't know where to start.

'We know so little about each other...' Her cheeks flushed as he gave a low, sardonic laugh. 'Well, apart from *that* aspect of our relationship, I don't even know the simplest, most ordinary things—like what size of shoes you take, the sort of music you like, or your birthday...'

He put his arm about her shoulder, his eyes crinkling in lazy amusement. 'Size ten, Mozart, and the seventeenth of November,' he answered promptly.

'Oh, dear—that means you're a Scorpio. Aren't they supposed to be very...'

'Difficult to live with?' he grinned. 'Never mind, darling, I'm sure that you'll be able to handle me with one hand tied behind your back!'

'Mmm...' Polly murmured, not at all sure of being able to do any such thing, and grateful that he had interrupted before she'd completed her sentence. She had been going to say something quite different: words such as 'lustful' and 'passionate' having come quickly to mind. And she wasn't far wrong about his star sign, she thought, her stomach clenching as a quick, lightning flash of pleasure zigzagged through her body at the recollection of their earlier, tempestuous lovemaking.

'Tell me some more about yourself,' she said breathlessly as they reached the river, grateful to be able to sit down on a fallen log and rest her legs, which felt unaccountably weak and wobbly.

'Well, let's see—I love the smell of the earth after rain, driving fast, expensive sports cars, sexy redheads—of course!—and I'm also nuts about horses. As for what I dislike...' He paused, pursing his lips in thought. 'English custard, jazz, paying too much income tax and, most of all, those directors who don't believe that actors can act, and insist on telling them—every damn second—exactly what to do,' he added grimly.

'What made you decide to go into films?'

He smiled. 'It certainly wasn't a conscious decision. In fact, with my parents both involved in breeding racehorses, I learned to ride before I could walk, and grew up wanting to be a jockey. Unfortunately, I was well over six feet tall by the time I was sixteen, and however much I starved myself I couldn't seem to get down to the necessary weight. I still hadn't decided what I wanted to do with my life, when my parents were killed in a road crash, leaving nothing but a pile of debts.' He shrugged his broad shoulders. 'I suppose that if they'd been alive I might have gone to college, but, since there was no money left after I'd settled all the outstanding bills, I decided to set off across the country to make my fortune.'

'You were awfully young to be wandering around America on your own, weren't you?' Polly looked at him in concern. 'Didn't you have any relatives you could go and stay with?'

James shook his head. 'Nope. I was an only child of only children, both my grandfathers had been killed in the war, and I don't remember hearing any mention of a grandmother. Anyway, I drifted around the States, doing just about every job under the sun, and then I bumped into an old school-friend whose parents had moved to California. We were both flat broke at the time, and he suggested that we could make a few dollars by signing on as extras on a Western movie being shot on location nearby. And that's it, really.'

'Oh, come on! You're just getting to the interesting part!' she protested.

'You don't really want to hear...'

'Yes, I certainly do,' she said firmly.

He sighed. 'OK, but I warn that that it's a very boring story. Basically, what happened was that the director of the film spotted my ability with horses, and thought I looked right for a small part the scriptwriters had just added for the temperamental leading lady. I didn't know much about acting then, of course, but I did well enough on that picture to be chosen for another, with a slightly larger part, and things just snowballed on from there.'

'Hmm... I noticed that bit about the leading lady,' Polly muttered unhappily. 'Did you... I mean, do you often...?'

James gave a rueful laugh. 'I knew I was going to regret this conversation!' he said, coming over to sit down on the log and putting his arms about her.

'My darling, I was only twenty-two when I got my first chance in movies, and I'm now thirty-four,' he said quietly. 'I'd be lying if I said that I haven't had many girlfriends during the past twelve years—some of whom I've slept with and some I haven't. And I'm sure, if you're honest, you wouldn't want a guy who hadn't played the field. After all, how else would I have known, with absolute certainty, that you were the girl for me?'

'Well . . . I suppose it's silly of me to worry about what you did in the past,' she muttered.

'Yes, it is—and I definitely don't want to know about any of your old boyfriends, either,' he said firmly. 'Professionally speaking, I've always made it a rule never to get involved with any of my leading ladies; quite apart from anything else, those sort of romances can cause the most God-awful havoc and mayhem on a film set.'

He put up a hand and turned her face towards him, his brilliant blue eyes gazing intently down into hers. 'I love you, my sweet Polly, and I can promise that I'll give you no cause to doubt my love, either now or in the future.' His voice was raw and husky with emotion, his arms tightening around her as his mouth closed over hers in a kiss of rampant possession.

When he finally raised his head, she lay breathless in his arms, her senses dazed and drugged by the magic of his kiss and the hard, lean masculinity of the flesh so close to her own. James, too, seemed to be having a little trouble with his breathing, and it was some moments before he found his voice.

'OK,' he said at last. 'This is where the kissing has to stop—for the moment, anyway—because we've got a great many arrangements to make, and very little time in which to get everything organised.'

'Things such as a special marriage licence?' she murmured.

'Mm-hmm. I had a devil of a time getting that piece of paper, although Marty did most of the work while I was in Rome. But it was worth all the hassle, because we can now get married in three days' time.'

'James! I'll never make it!' she exclaimed with an incredulous laugh.

'Sure, you will. I've already been in touch with your local preacher, since I needed a letter from him to obtain the licence, and it's all set for eleven o'clock on Friday morning.'

'Oh, really...?' she drawled, her spine stiffening as she sat upright, inching away from the arm placed casually around her waist. If there was one thing she *really* disliked, it was being ordered around and told what she could and couldn't do. On top of which, she *definitely* didn't care for the way in which he seemed to be assuming control of her life, and she might as well nip it in the bud as quickly as possible.

'I'm sorry you didn't consult me before making your plans,' she said in a cool voice. 'Unfortunately, it just so happens that I'm doing something else that day.'

'No, you're not,' he said flatly, grasping hold of her hands and turning her around to face him. 'I knew we'd come to this sort of crunch, sooner or later, so I guess this is where I'd better lay it right on the line for you, Polly. While I have no intention of interfering in any way with your running of the farm—that's your business, and you obviously do it damn well—I want you to realise that

I've every intention of being the boss in my own home.'

She gasped. 'What do you mean, your home? It's *my* house and farm—and don't you forget it!'

'And why don't you calm down—and start using your brain?' he retorted in a hard voice. 'OK, now let's take it from the top,' he added as she fumed silently beside him. 'Do you want to leave Winterfloods?'

'No, of course I don't!'

'That's exactly what I thought. So, if we are to be married, it follows that I must come and live with you here, at the farm. Right?'

Polly opened her mouth, and then closed it again as she tried to clear her mind and concentrate on what he was saying. Events had moved so fast that she hadn't really had the opportunity, or the time, to work out the various ramifications of their marriage. 'Do you mind?' she muttered. 'Coming to live here at the farm, I mean? I don't suppose it's the usual way of doing things, but ...'

'Relax!' he said firmly. 'I have no hang-ups about moving in with you. In fact, I've been looking for a rich wife for years, and now I'm going to be a kept man—fantastic!'

'You don't really mean that ... do you?' She looked at him doubtfully.

He smiled, and leaned forward to kiss her freckled nose. 'No, I was only kidding! I know that you're a wealthy girl, but I reckon I can still top you by a million or two. However, I fear we are straying from the point,' he added, the smile dying from his face.

'Oh, lord, you weren't really serious about all that he-man, macho, "I'm the boss" nonsense?'

'Perfectly serious.'

'But that's ridiculous! We're living in the twentieth century, for heaven's sake. Haven't you heard about sexual equality?' she demanded angrily.

'Sure I have, and I'm all for it.' He gave her a bland smile. 'I'm going to have the ultimate and final say in our personal and private affairs—and you can run your business, and the rest of your life in any way you want. How's that for equality, hmm?'

'Not only are you a male chauvinist pig—but you're a hard, domineering bastard!' she retorted fiercely.

'Oh, ho—look who's talking!' he drawled, his lips twitching with amusement as he stared down into her stormy eyes. 'You're one very tough lady, Polly, and if I gave you half a chance you'd instinctively try to walk all over me with your bare feet. Darling, I love your independent streak and your strength of character, but that doesn't mean that I'm prepared to let you push me around. So, if anyone's wearing the trousers in our home— you'd better face the fact that it's going to be me! Got the message?'

'Loud and clear!' she ground out bitterly, her eyes searching his stern, unrelenting features for some sign of weakness. The damned man—who in the hell did he think he was, dictating to her like this? 'I'm going to be the boss,' indeed! For two pins, she'd tell him to get lost, and...

For a moment there was a total hiatus in her mind as she realised that in telling James to 'get lost', she was in imminent danger of throwing away all her future hopes of happiness. Rightly or wrongly, he had laid down the terms on which their marriage would be based and, if she didn't accept them, what then? She knew with absolute certainty that he was her first, last and only love; that even if there were to be only these few, short weeks of bliss, she would still never, ever want another man. Her stomach churned, and she felt quite sick at just the mere thought of losing James. *And for—what?* It was, after all, a very trivial matter. Any woman worth her salt ought to be able to get her own way; surely all it took was a judicious mixture of low cunning and feminine wiles?

Watching the various thoughts chasing themselves across her expressive face, James was well aware of the fierce internal struggle Polly was waging with herself.

'Well?' he murmured.

'OK—you win,' she sighed, avoiding his eyes as he placed a hand beneath her chin, tilting her face up towards him.

'I don't want to win—I just want parity.' He gave low, sardonic laugh. 'And I can see I'm going to have a hell of a job even trying to get that!' he added, drawing her closely into his arms. 'Never mind, sweetheart, just think of all the fun you're going to have over the next twenty-five years, plotting and conniving to get your own way.'

'I was just—er—thinking about that,' she muttered, grinning sheepishly up through her eyelashes at the handsome, tanned face only inches away from her own.

'I know. And I also know that I love you very much,' he whispered softly as his mouth possessed hers, and she melted beneath the sensual magic of his lips, abandoning in the erotic fervour of his kiss all thoughts of the future. The only reality was now, this moment, when the world held nothing but themselves and their deeply passionate need of each other.

The next three days flew by at the speed of light. Never, in all her life, had Polly been involved in making so many vitally important decisions, or so many complicated arrangements, in such a short space of time. As far as the farm itself was concerned, her cheesemaker, Jim Moxon, had proved to be a tower of strength.

'Of course I can run the place while you're away on your honeymoon,' he had said, hardly pausing as he checked through the cow's record sheets. 'How long do you reckon you're going to be away?'

'About two weeks, I think, although it might be a bit longer.'

'Well, as far as I'm concerned, you can stay away for the next two months,' Jim said briskly. 'Now that we've dried off the cows, and there's no milk for making cheese, I've got lots of time to oversee the men when they combine those two fields of barley. It's all systems go when the cows begin calving, of course, but until then it's no problem. Mr Linklater seems a very nice bloke,' he added gruffly. 'I hope you'll both be very happy.'

And so do I! Polly thought, recalling Jim's words as she drove back to the farm from her hurried shopping trip to Shrewsbury. With only one day to go before she was married to the man of her dreams, she knew she ought to be feeling on top of the world. Unfortunately, after her furious argument with James last night, she was feeling confused and despondent.

He really was being totally unreasonable, she told herself for the umpteenth time. It was extremely unfair of him to expect her to go off with him on a short honeymoon, and then meekly return alone to Winterfloods, while he filmed the location shots in the Malaysian jungle for his new movie, *None But The Brave*. Since James had taken no notice of her strong protests, she had been forced to temporarily drop the subject but, if he thought she was prepared to put up with being abandoned by her new husband so soon after their marriage, he was very much mistaken!

Exactly how she was going to persuade James to let her go with him on location was something she hadn't yet worked out, and she was still wrestling with the problem as she stood staring down at her open suitcase later that afternoon. Apart from telling her to pack a few bikinis, he had been remarkably silent as to where they were going on their honeymoon. But maybe during the next two weeks of hot days—and, hopefully, even hotter nights!— *plus* the ammunition provided by her new, skimpily cut and decidedly provocative bikinis, she might persuade him to change his mind.

Elsie's reaction to her newly purchased swimwear was definitely encouraging.

'*Miss Polly!* You're never going to wear them nasty, rude things?' she exclaimed in horrified tones as she came into the bedroom. 'Downright disgusting, I call it!' she added, gingerly picking up one of the small scraps of material. 'Still...' She gave a dramatic sigh. 'Your James tells me that all you young girls wear them bikinis nowadays—and, seeing as how it's your honeymoon, I suppose it's all right and proper.'

Polly gave a snort of cynical laughter, quickly converting it into a cough as she turned away to hide her grin. Goodness knew, James was loaded with charm, but how he'd managed to get around Elsie quite so quickly, she had absolutely no idea. In fact, Polly thought sourly, she was getting just a little tired of constantly being told that she was a lucky girl, and of hearing her fiancé's virtues trumpeted forth with such frequency.

'Have you decided what you're wearing at this here wedding?' Elsie's voice broke into her thoughts. 'And have you got hold of your stepma yet? Being so far away in Australia, both she and the Squire will be dang upset if they don't hear from you before you waltzes up the aisle—that I do know.'

'I keep phoning and leaving messages at their hotel, but they haven't yet called back. So, for goodness' sake—stop nagging!' Polly snapped, and then immediately felt contrite at taking her increasing feelings of anxiety out of Elsie. 'I'm sorry,' she mumbled. 'I don't know what's wrong with me, but I seem to be feeling so sick and tense all the time.'

'Don't you worry, my duck, it's just wedding nerves,' Elsie said, coming over to put a comforting arm about her shoulders. 'You'll be right as a trivet tomorrow, just you see.'

'I hope so,' Polly sighed, picking up a cardboard box and pulling out the cream silk dress by Jasper Conran, which she had bought in Shrewsbury. 'What do you think? Will it do?'

'You'll look a right treat in that,' Elsie said, nodding her approval as she viewed the tightly fitted bodice and the full, three-quarter-length skirt falling from a dropped waistline. 'Your James was wanting to know what flowers you'd like—and I reckon that cream and pink roses would be just about right.'

'Hmm, fine...' Polly murmured, wishing with all her heart that she could get the next twenty-four hours out of the way.

During the last three days she had been rushing about like one demented, desperately trying to cram into the short space of time which she had been allotted by James, details and arrangements which would normally have taken her three weeks. It wouldn't have been so bad if, at the end of each exhausting day, she had been able to relax in the warmth and security of James's arms. However, upon Elsie's return to the farm, James had insisted on them observing the proprieties. 'I don't want to upset the old girl,' he had explained. 'Her generation is a lot more strait-laced than ours and, since we're going to be spending the rest of our lives together, I guess you and I can hack a few more nights on our own, hmm?' he had added, leaving her gently but firmly at the door of her own bedroom.

Left alone to face the long, solitary nights, her body gripped by an ever-increasing nervous tension from which she found it difficult to relax, there seemed little Polly could do to prevent herself from being racked by hideous doubts and uncertainties.

She and James loved each other, but was that enough to face all the problems which must lie ahead of them? Not only were they very different people, but their life-styles were so diametrically opposed to each other. In fact, by marrying a man about whom she knew so little, was she in danger of making a disastrous, and monumentally foolish, mistake?

CHAPTER SIX

IT WAS well past the normal time for breakfast when Polly walked slowly into the Palm Court of Raffles Hotel. It was one of the strategies she had devised lately, as if by rising late and retiring early to her suite, she could somehow persuade the days to pass that much quicker.

It didn't really make any difference, of course. She was just as effectively trapped here as those little songbirds in their wicker cages, hanging from the green and white striped awning over the veranda edging the tropical garden of Singapore's world-famous hotel.

Giving her order to the hovering waiter, she leaned back in her chair and stared moodily into space, hardly noticing the mynah birds strutting arrogantly back and forth over the grass, the trailing fronds of frangipani and bougainvillaea which rustled in the morning breeze, or the brilliant plumage of the golden orioles as they flashed between the fan-shaped palm trees surrounding the well manicured lawn.

What was she going to do? Ever since yesterday, after the phone call from her stepmother, Alicia, and the belated realisation of exactly why she had been feeling so tired and apathetic lately—not to mention those dreadful bouts of nausea—she had known that she must make a decision, one way or another. It was six weeks since she and James had got married, and for the last three of those weeks she had seen and heard nothing of her new husband. He had told her that communications would be difficult, but try as she might—and she'd spent most of yesterday on the telephone—she had been unable to get through to the remote jungle area where he, and the rest of the film unit, were shooting the location scenes for the new movie. In fact, to all intents and purposes, she might just as well be back at Winterfloods. And it didn't help to know that, even if she did eventually manage to contact James, he wouldn't have an ounce of sympathy. In fact, she thought gloomily, he would undoubtedly rub salt in her wounds by saying, 'I told you so.' And he would be right. He *had* told her how it would be, but she simply hadn't been prepared to listen—determined not to hear about anything that might intrude or impinge upon their own private world of happiness.

From the very first moment of her wedding day, when she had woken to find a huge diamond ring and a wonderfully warm, tender letter from James on her bedside table, all her doubts and uncertainties had vanished like the morning mist. Defying convention and Elsie's superstitious warnings, they had driven together to the village church and, as she and James had walked slowly up the aisle beneath the stone, vaulted arches of the old Norman church, she had been radiant with joy and happiness. The service itself, a very simple affair with just Elsie and James's agent, Marty, as their two witnesses, had been deeply moving, and when they had left the church she was still in such a daze of elation and delight that not even the completely unexpected appearance of a battery of Press reporters and photographers could spoil the day. On a total high, she had merely laughed at James's anger with Marty. 'I need this sort of publicity like a dog needs fleas!' he had snapped. Possibly the bottle of champagne, which they had consumed in the chauffeur-driven limousine taking them to the airport, had contributed to her sense of blissful unreality, but not even the presence of yet more photographers and autograph hunters, nor the long and tiring flight, could dent her trancelike state of euphoria.

James's choice of a honeymoon location had been nothing less than inspired. Situated on the relatively unknown east coast of Malaysia, overlooking a long stretch of deserted beach edging the South China Sea, the small, luxurious hotel at Tanjongjara contained only a few other guests— mainly Chinese and Malay, who spoke not a word of English—and had proved to be a secret haven of utter peace and tranquillity.

Time had seemed to have no meaning during those hot sunny days, which they had spent swimming in the warm sea or walking hand in hand over the white sandy beach. And their lovemaking, beneath the star-lit, velvety darkness of those warm, tropical nights, had been so breathtaking, so indescribably perfect that she felt as though she had been transported to Paradise.

Polly had always known that it couldn't last for ever, but the arrival of the telex from Marty, towards the end of their second week of honeymoon, had seemed to herald the entry of the snake into their private Garden of Eden. Not that she really thought of James's agent in such reptilian terms, of course. In fact she had liked the small, fat man whom James had assured her was one of the best agents in the business. He obviously had a job to do, and he seemed to be doing it very well, if the ever-increasing flow of phone calls and telexed instructions were anything to go by. However, as Polly found herself being forced to spend more and more time on her own, sitting disconsolately on the beach while James and Marty conducted their incomprehensible telephone conversations, she found herself fervently wishing that the agent would get off the phone and out of her life.

'OK. Thanks, Marty—I'll call you from Singapore,' James said, putting down the phone as she entered their room one morning.

'Singapore?' she queried uneasily.

'It seems the producers and the money men in New York are trying to wriggle out of part of my contract—and I'm sure as hell not putting up with that nonsense!' he said with a grim smile. 'So—get your skates on and start packing,' he added, pulling their suitcases out of a cupboard. 'We've only got an hour to catch the plane.'

'But, if there's a problem, why can't we stay here? Why do we have to go to Singapore?' she wailed, sinking miserably down on to the bed as he began throwing his clothes into the cases.

'Because that's where the action is,' he retorted tersely. 'And for God's sake, hurry up! We don't have much time.'

After the peaceful, quiet tempo of Eastern Malaysia, Singapore proved to be very different. If James was looking for 'action', this bustling, modern city was exactly the right place, Polly thought, as their taxi took them from the magnificently spacious Changi airport through the crowded streets, with their Manhattan-like skyscrapers towering over the banks, the smart shops selling everything under the sun, and the hawkers' open-air food stalls where exotic dishes were being cooked and sold to the passers by.

When they eventually arrived at Raffles Hotel, Polly's dismay at the abrupt termination of their honeymoon was considerably soothed by the warmth of their welcome, and she was entranced by the faded grandeur of the graceful, ornate building which still conveyed the atmosphere of Britain's colonial past. Once installed in their suite of rooms in the writer's annex—commemorating the famous names who had stayed at the hotel, such as Rudyard Kipling, Somerset Maugham and Noël Coward—she and James explored the old hotel. When they finally sat down to dinner in the Palm Court, Polly had difficulty in keeping her face straight.

'Honestly, this place is an absolute hoot!' she exclaimed with a wide grin. 'What with "Cad's Alley" and the "Tiffin Room", I expect to be called "Memsahib" any minute. It's just as though we had somehow entered a time-warp, and been transported back to over fifty years ago.'

'It certainly makes a change from...' James's words were interrupted as a trio of Chinese violinists in the far corner suddenly began playing 'When I'm Calling You-ooo-ooo...' and Polly promptly collapsed with laughter.

Thinking about the episode later, she realised that it was positively the last time that she had the occasion to laugh, or to find anything even remotely amusing, for the next three weeks. But, unaware of what fate had in store for her, she had merely looked up with interest as a tall, burly man approached their table.

'Hi, Link—you son of a gun!' he boomed, slapping James on the back and pulling up a chair to their table. 'We were all wondering when you'd turn up. Chuck, Ben and the others are out, sampling the delights of the luscious girls at the Tropicana, but I sure don't blame you for wining and dining this little lady!' He winked at Polly and gave James a sharp dig in the ribs.

James gave Polly a rueful smile. 'This, although I'm ashamed to say so, is a fellow actor friend of mine, Rod Stevens. And, for your information,' he added, turning to Rod, 'I'd better tell you straight away that the "little lady" happens to be my wife.'

'Wow! No kidding?' The large man gave a shout of laughter. 'Well, this *definitely* calls for a celebration,' he roared, signalling to a hovering waiter. 'Champagne, my man—and step on it! I'm crazy about this place,' he confided to Polly. 'I really go for this British Raj type of caper.'

'Yes, I agree that the atmosphere is very...'

'Aha—I can tell from her accent that the little lady is British, too—fantastic!' Rod continued, his voice resounding around the Palm Court as if he was using a megaphone. 'Well, well—who'd have guessed that old Link Jameson, the romantic heartthrob of millions of women, would finally succumb to the dreaded ball and chain! Hey... does Melody

know you've got married?' he asked, rolling his eyes
and wheezing with laughter as James's lips tightened
into a grim line.

'My marriage concerns no one but Polly and
myself,' he retorted coldly.

'OK, OK—I get the message!' Rod held up his
huge hands in a gesture of surrender. 'So, tell me,
what's going on? We're all here—plus the camera
crew, of course—but I hear tell there's a delay in
shooting because of some hassle about money, back
in New York. You know anything about that?'

James shook his head. 'We've only just flown in
here today, and you're the first person I've talked
to since we arrived.'

Polly was just opening her mouth to remind him
about his phone call with Marty, when she caught
the warning flash in his steely blue eyes, and quickly
closed it again. What on earth was he up to? He
hadn't exactly lied to this man, Rod, but he hadn't
told him the truth, either. However, she didn't get
a chance to question James privately about his
strange evasion, as the waiter arrived with the
champagne, closely followed by a large group of
men complaining loudly about the lack of vice in
the nightclub they had just visited.

It had been a long, tiring day, and by the time
she had been introduced as James's new wife—
which immediately produced more congratulations
and orders for yet more champagne—Polly could
feel herself wilting. It wasn't so much the crowd of
strangers all talking at the top of their voices which
was so confusing, but the fact that they seemed to
be speaking an unknown language. A tall, thin man
was gesturing wildly. ' . . . so I told him the light

was getting too yellow, and we'd never match the scene:..' while Rod and a man he called Chuck were immersed in a long, technical discussion about 'off-takes', 'master shots' and 'answer prints'.

She was just trying to signal James that she was tired, and would like to go back to their suite, when she realised that the noise had suddenly abated. Turning her head, she saw walking slowly towards their table one of the loveliest girls she had ever seen in her life. Polly might have been feeling exhausted, but she wasn't too weary not to recognise, in the hushed and almost reverent silence, an overwhelming tribute to the sultry voluptuousness of the ravishingly beautiful woman.

'My darling James—where *have* you been?' the woman breathed in a low, husky voice, posing for a moment so that the assembled company could appreciate her long, black hair rippling down over deeply tanned skin, and the skintight, white strapless dress which left little to the imagination, barely clinging to the full sensuous curves of her breasts. And then, placing her arms about his head, she bent down to give James a long, passionate kiss, before sinuously sliding down to sit on his lap.

Polly could scarcely believe her eyes. She'd heard about the goings-on among Hollywood film stars— but this was ridiculous! If there was one thing she *really* hated, she quickly decided, it was tiny women with pocket Venus figures who didn't know when they weren't wanted! She could feel her cheeks flushing, her chest almost bursting as she struggled not to scream, Get your hands off my husband! at the woman who was now snuggling up closer to

James, and burying her fingers in his thick, dark hair.

Polly was saved from making an exhibition of herself, as she became aware of everyone's eyes swivelling in her direction, their faces avid with interest and the anticipation of an explosive scene. I won't give them the satisfaction! she told herself grimly, clenching her hands so tightly that the nails bit into her palms. Forcing herself to remain silent, she noticed that James, for his part, didn't seem to be in the least embarrassed. Coolly but firmly disentangling himself from the arms clasped about his head, he calmly set the woman on her feet before rising from his chair.

'Go and play your games with someone else, Melody,' he said quietly, before coming around to where Polly was sitting rigidly upright, and fuming with indignation. Taking her hand, he raised it to his lips. 'My wife and I have only been married for two weeks,' he said with a bland smile. 'So I'm sure you'll all understand if we now say good-night—and go to bed!'

His words broke the tension, and a ripple of laughter ran around the group as he placed his arm firmly about Polly's waist, and led her away from the table. As they walked across the garden towards their suite of rooms, Polly was conscious of the girl's hot, dark eyes following their progress.

'Who on earth was that extraordinary woman?' she demanded when they reached the sanctuary of their bedroom.

'Melody Grant? She's playing the female lead in the movie. God, I'm tired...' James yawned as he shrugged off his jacket.

'Well, I hope you're going to make it absolutely clear to her that she doesn't have a starring role in our marriage!' Polly remarked bitterly.

He laughed. 'Relax, sweetheart. You don't want to take any notice of her—she's a complete nutcase.'

'Humph!' Polly gave a loud snort of derision. She didn't think Melody was at all nutty. That dangerous harpy obviously knew *exactly* what she wanted, and it looked as if James was at the top of her shopping list!

'There's no need for you to be jealous,' he murmured, a mocking smile on his lips as he walked over and took her into his arms.

'I'm not!' she protested breathlessly, her heart beginning to pound as she glimpsed the naked desire in the blue eyes gleaming down at her. Leaning weakly against his broad chest, savouring the warmth of his body through the thin silk shirt, she trembled as his hands began caressing the soft swell of her hips.

'I don't want any other woman,' he whispered softly, trailing his mouth slowly down the delicate curve of her cheek. 'Only you, my sweet Polly,' he breathed, bestowing a long, lingering kiss on her softly parted lips as he raised a hand and began undoing her zip...

Polly winced, her stomach giving an ominous lurch as the waiter put a plate of fried eggs and bacon in front of her. Oh, lord—what on earth had possessed her to order that sort of breakfast? Carefully waiting until the servant had turned to serve another table, she pushed the plate away and surreptitiously covered it with a spare napkin. 'Out of sight, out of mind,' she thought as she remembered one of Elsie's favourite sayings, and was suddenly assailed by an acute wave of homesickness for Winterfloods, a desperate longing to put her head on the old housekeeper's shoulder and bawl her eyes out.

How incredibly stupid she'd been! It wasn't until she'd received that phone call yesterday from Alicia that she had finally realised why she'd been feeling so ill lately. Although, of course, it had been wonderful to hear from her stepmother at long last, and to learn that she and Giles were back in England.

'We're so sorry not to have been able to get in touch with you before now. And it wasn't until Elsie got your postcard today, from Singapore, that we knew where you were,' Alicia had said, explaining that she had been taken ill while they were staying with friends in Australia, and Giles had immediately decided that they should return to England.

'Darling Polly—fancy you marrying a film star!' Alicia's familiar gurgle of laughter had suddenly made Polly feel extraordinarily homesick. 'Elsie is quite besotted with your handsome husband, and Giles and I can't wait to meet him. I'm sure you must be ecstatically happy. Are you having a wonderful honeymoon?'

'Oh yes, absolutely fantastic!' Polly had replied, doing her best to sound madly enthusiastic, before quickly changing the subject. 'But what's this about you being ill?'

'Well, as it turned out, I wasn't exactly ill...' Alicia had hesitated and then given a low, self-conscious laugh. 'It's quite ridiculous, especially at my age, but after having given up all hope—it now seems that I'm expecting a baby!'

'That's wonderful news, and Giles must be over the moon!' Polly had said excitedly, before reminding her stepmother that, at thirty years of age, she was only four years older than herself, and therefore not exactly ancient! However, after listening to the list of symptoms, which Alicia had mistaken for some obscure stomach complaint, Polly had put down the phone at the end of their conversation with a dark, heavy presentiment which had immediately hardened into certainty as soon as she did some simple mental arithmetic.

She had spent a thoroughly miserable night—and was still feeling absolutely shattered this morning. Alicia had mentioned the word 'ridiculous' but what could be more farcical or ludicrous than the present situation? Who had ever heard of a stepmother and stepdaughter, both expecting a baby at the same time?

Blinking rapidly against the weak tears which filled her eyes, she fished a handkerchief out of her bag and furiously blew her nose, before pouring herself another cup of tea. It was no good getting upset, or castigating herself for having been so caught up in the euphoria of her love affair, and her subsequent rush to the altar with James, that she had neglected to take any precautions. Clearly, it was now far too late to begin thinking about methods of birth control, she told herself grimly.

How long would it be before she began putting on weight? she wondered, placing a trembling hand on her stomach, which was still as flat as a pancake. She'd have to go and see a doctor, of course, but

the thought of having a baby was somehow so
extraordinary—and frightening—that she hadn't
yet come to terms with all the implications of approaching motherhood. It was a subject about
which she knew less than nothing, and she had no
idea how James would react to the news. Would he
still love her when she was heavily pregnant, and
staggering around like a vast ship in full sail?
Although, after the awful week they'd spent together here at Raffles, which had culminated in that
dreadful quarrel, and the ominous silence ever
since, she wasn't sure how he'd feel when he discovered that she was carrying his child.

He had told her to ignore Melody and, goodness
knew, she'd tried to keep well away from the horrid
woman. An intention that was easier said than
done. Maybe if James had been more in evidence,
she would have found it easier to avoid his leading
lady, who took every opportunity to make it quite
clear to Polly that she and James had been lovers
in the past—what Melody constantly referred to as
'our tumultuous affair'—confidently asserting that
James would soon grow tired of his new wife and
return to his old flame.

However, during the first four days after they
had arrived at the hotel, James had been virtually
non-existent. Rising while she was still asleep, he
hadn't returned to the hotel until very late at night,
and had obstinately refused to say where he'd been.
Desperately trying to ignore her dark suspicion and
jealousy—if James wasn't making love to Melody,
where was he?—she felt an absolute fool at being
so conspicuously abandoned in the hotel on her
own, and fed up with constantly being asked where

her husband was by the rest of the film crew. The director of the movie, Donald Buckley, had been particularly anxious to know James's whereabouts, and it wasn't until after a conversation with Rod Stevens, the actor whom she'd met on her first evening at Raffles, that she began to have some inkling of what James was up to.

'Poor old Donald—our esteemed director is tearing his hair out by the handful!' he grinned.

'Why should he do that?' she had asked dully, not really caring about the answer one way or another.

'Well, a little bird tells me that the studio signed up Link for this production, without looking too clearly at the small print in his contract!'

'So?'

'So—*kapow*!' Rod roared with laughter. 'I hear tell that Link's contract says he has a five-per-cent piece of the gross and, since they reckon this picture is going to be a smash hit, that little bit of carelessness is going to cost them a small fortune! Oh, God—I just love seeing the sharks getting bitten for a change!' he added with another booming laugh.

Polly looked at him in bewilderment. 'I honestly don't understand what any of you film people are talking about most of the time. What is a piece of gross, or whatever? And, if there's some problem with James's—er—Link's contract, why should your director be upset?'

'Aha! I wondered if Link was keeping you in the dark, along with the rest of us. He sure plays his cards close to his chest, doesn't he? Never you mind, honey,' Rod said quickly, as he saw her flush with the mortification of discovering that, despite being married to him, James didn't trust her any further than he did his own colleagues. 'You just sit back, and old Uncle Rod will tell you all about the intricacies of movie finance. OK?'

'OK . . .' she said unhappily.

'Right, let's start with the basic fact that we actors get a sum of money—as outlined in our contracts—for each picture we work on. And, as we become more successful, our agents begin negotiating for a piece of the net profits of the box-office returns as well. However, the money men in New York have a really fancy way of doing their bookkeeping, so, while it's good for your career, statuswise, it's very rare to make any money from a share of the net profits,' he said with a wry smile.

'So why bother making the deal in the first place?'

'Ah . . .' he grinned. 'Because the next step up, both in terms of career and finance, is to obtain a share of the *gross* profits—what's commonly called a piece of the gross. However, all this high finance doesn't affect actors like me. We're just damn glad to get hold of a good part in a picture, and grateful for whatever our agents can get us. The stars who can demand a gross share of the profits on a picture are very few and far between. In fact, I'd say it's quite a small, exclusive club. But once you've joined it—oh boy! You're talking about a helluva lot of *real* money—if the movie's successful, of course.'

Polly frowned. 'And how do you know whether this film *None But the Brave* will be a success?'

'You never can tell, which is half the fun with this business,' he shrugged. 'The only query is—

seeing as how we've had *The Deer Hunter* and *The Killing Fields*, not to mention old Stallone rampaging around as Rambo—whether stories about brave American soldiers escaping through the Vietnamese jungle have been done to death. However, it ought to be a success: it's got a first-class script, a good director, and with Link in the starring role it should be a smash hit.'

'Is he—er—is my husband a good actor?'

Rod looked at her in astonishment. 'Lady—where have you been living lately? Of course he's good. In fact, with a decent director and a halfway good script, he's damn good verging on brilliant. He didn't get that Oscar nomination for his part in *Indian Summer* for nothing, you know!'

Polly stared at him in silence for a moment. The trouble was that she really didn't know. She was beginning to suspect that she knew nothing about James, who certainly had never mentioned anything about an Oscar nomination—which even she knew was the highest accolade in the motion-picture business. However, since Rod seemed prepared to gossip about the movie industry, she might as well try and find out as much as possible.

'Thanks for...well, for explaining all that money business, but I still don't understand why the details of my husband's contract should matter to the director of this picture you're making?'

'It's dead simple,' Rod said with a grin. 'If what I hear is right, it seems the studio finance boys woke up the other day, and discovered—shock, horror, dismay!—that thanks to his cast-iron contract Link was going to be getting his hands on a large slice of their profits. They couldn't get out of the contract, so they reckoned that it would be cheaper to sack him from the picture, and try and get someone else. He'd sue them, of course, but they'd be better off financially in the long run. With me so far?'

'Yes. I must say they sound a fairly horrid bunch of people.'

'Damn right!' he laughed. 'Anyway, things started going wrong when no other star was immediately available, which has slowed down the action and pushed up the production costs—bad financial news for the studio! On top of which, the director, Donald Buckley, is also putting pressure on the studio. He was always mad keen to have Link in the picture, and seeing you around the hotel all the time—but never being able to find Link and pin him down for a long discussion—well, it's slowly driving him up the wall!'

'So what's going to happen now?' she asked.

He shrugged. 'Your guess is as good as mine. According to Melody, the word is that Link has issued an ultimatum. Either the studio decide to honour his contract within the next forty-eight hours—in which case we can begin shooting the picture—or else he's going to issue a writ in the courts for breaking his contract. Whatever happens, Link's got them over a barrel.' Rod lay back in his chair and stretched his large frame. 'I reckon your old man is one smooth operator!'

Isn't he just! she thought grimly, as she wandered around a large department store later in the day. There were several disturbing points which had been raised in her mind by Rod, and she had felt far too restless to stay cooped up in the hotel. For instance, it didn't take the IQ of a genius to realise what James had been up to: he'd obviously been using her presence in the hotel to put pressure on both his director and the studio. Neither had she missed the reference to Melody knowing exactly what James was planning to do. He clearly thought his wife was so dumb that she had to be left in blissful ignorance of his plans! Why the hell couldn't he have trusted her?

Polly was so cross and angry with James that when she saw his photograph on a huge poster, she thought for a moment that she was hallucinating. But no—there it was, stretched across the top of a cinema, proudly proclaiming in letters six feet high:

LINK JAMESON
and
Melody Grant in
INDIAN SUMMER
Exciting Adventure! . . . A Torrid Romance!

Almost as though she was sleepwalking, Polly found herself crossing the wide, busy street and approaching the foyer of the large, air-conditioned cinema. Everyone else seemed to know everything about her husband, so she might as well try and catch up, she thought as she purchased a ticket and entered the dark auditorium. When she left, over two hours later, she was in such a daze that she had to have several strong cups of coffee in a nearby café before she felt able to call a taxi and return to the hotel.

Lying alone in their huge double bed later that night, she was still trying to sort out the confusion and chaos in her mind.

It was as if she was somehow married to two different people. The public Link Jameson, and the
private James Linklater. Both quite separate personalities. In the film she had just seen, Link and/
or James had played a renegade soldier from the
Deep South, who was adopted by a tribe of North
American Indians, fell in love with a beautiful
Indian girl—Melody—and led the tribe in their vain
quest for new land and pastures, before dying
bravely in defence of justice, right and freedom.
The story had been hardly earthshaking, but even
with her limited experience of movie-going it was
obvious that Link/James had given a great performance. For long stretches of the time, she had
become so immersed in the story, she had forgotten
that it was her husband up there on the silver screen.
And then, with the use of a familiar gesture, she
would be reminded that it was not just an actor
who was making hot, passionate love to Melody
Grant, but the man she had married only two weeks
ago...

She had fallen asleep before James returned to
their room that night, and the next morning she
had awoken to find him already on the phone to
his agent.

'OK—it's all systems go,' he said after putting
down the receiver. 'The studio have caved in, and
we're all flying up to the location site this afternoon. Marty has arranged for your flight back to
England, and...'

'Marty can take a flying jump out of the window,
for all I care. And so can you!' she retorted angrily.
'I'm your wife—just in case you've forgotten that
small fact—and yet I've been treated as if I was

blind, deaf, dumb and a complete idiot. Why didn't you tell me what was going on?' she demanded furiously. 'Why didn't you trust me?'

'Calm down, sweetheart, there's no need to get so excited,' he said soothingly. 'Maybe I should have told you, but it was a very delicately balanced, difficult "game plan", and I couldn't take the risk of anyone tumbling what I was up to.'

'But, don't you see,' she waved her hands distractedly, 'I'm not "anyone"—I'm your wife!'

'Sure you are,' he murmured, busy putting letters and papers into his briefcase, and clearly not really listening to what she was saying.

'*James!*' she screamed at the top of her voice, and when she had his startled attention she tried to explain her deep confusion following her visit to the cinema yesterday, the sheer indignity she felt at having to put up with the spiteful comments of his leading lady, who also seemed to be his ex-girlfriend, and that she felt let down and betrayed by what she saw as his complete lack of trust. '...And I'm not going back to Winterfloods,' she said finally. 'I'm married to you, and my place is by your side.'

'Not on location, it's not!' he retorted curtly. 'And I simply don't understand any of this nonsense you've been spouting about my so-called public and private personalities,' he added sharply as she opened her mouth to protest. 'Nor do I want any more of that crap about Melody. I told you, back at the farm, that I don't mess around with my leading ladies.'

'Hah! Maybe someone ought to tell *her* that interesting bit of news?' Polly snarled. 'It's obviously time you two got together, and started learning to sing the same song...'

'Oh—for God's sake!'

'How about *The Melody Lingers On*? That sounds just *perfect*!' she shouted, almost shaking with overwhelming rage and fury.

Pale and tense, James stared grimly at her for a moment, and then his shoulders began to shake. 'Oh, sweetheart—what a crazy girl you are!' He gave a wry laugh as he put his arms about her trembling figure. 'There might be some items about which we could have a good, old-fashioned brawl—but I refuse to have a quarrel with you over a superbitch like Melody Grant. So cool it, huh?'

'B-but she said...'

'To hell with what she said! You're the one who's been yakking on about the importance of "trust" in our marriage—so how about trusting me for a change?' he grated bitterly. 'As far as I'm concerned, I've told you the truth, and if you don't believe me, then it's just too damn bad!'

Confused and shattered by the first real quarrel of their married life, Polly stared up into his hard blue eyes. He was right. There was little point in arguing about his relationship with his leading lady, and she desperately wanted—*needed*—to believe him. 'I'm sorry...' she whispered at last, and was rewarded as his arms tightened about her, and he possessed her lips in a long, passionate kiss.

For the rest of the morning they were both suffering from the aftermath of their quarrel, being very careful of what they said to each other, as if they were walking on eggshells. However, there seemed no way in which they could patch up the basic disagreement between them.

'I'm not taking you with me on location—and that's flat,' he said firmly. 'If you'd read the script, you'd know that I'm likely to be up to my waist in mud and water most of the time. It's going to be hell on wheels with leeches, mosquitoes and God knows what—and at the end of the day I'll be too tired to even say "hello". So go back to Winterfloods, Polly, and I'll join you there just as soon as I can.'

'I'm not going,' she retorted stubbornly. 'If you won't let me come with you, I'll stay on here in Singapore until you've finished filming. Besides, I heard some of the crew say that they get Sundays off, so you could always fly down here for the day, couldn't you?'

'Oh, God—I've never known such a damned obstinate woman!' he had groaned, raking his hands through his dark hair. 'All right, I give in. But I warn you that, since we're way behind schedule, the chances of my getting even one day off are so remote as to be laughable.'

And he'd been absolutely right, Polly thought with a glum sigh of resignation. She'd seen and heard nothing from him for the last three, dreadful weeks. Maybe she was suffering from some kind of mental sickness, but she hadn't been able to resist catching up on four more of James's films being shown at various cinemas in the city, which had merely resulted in making her feel even more miserable, if that were possible. How could she possibly explain to anyone, let alone James, what it felt like to see one's husband publicly making hot, torrid love to a succession of outstandingly beautiful women? And, because he was a good actor, and extremely convincing in his various roles, it somehow made it ten times worse. The basic concept, that her husband was a film star, and therefore public property, had been forcibly brought home to her only yesterday. Opening the *Straits Times* daily newspaper, she had idly glanced at the agony column on the women's page. Seeing a letter from a housewife who had written in to say that, while otherwise happily married, she was bored to tears by the predictable routine of her sex-life, Polly's eyes had widened in horror as she read the columnist's answer to the problem: ' . . . so why not try and imagine that you are making love to Link Jameson?' Gnashing her teeth and shredding the paper into tiny pieces had proved to be of little comfort, and had done nothing to help her ever-increasing sense of insecurity.

It was only pride which had kept her on at Raffles in the face of James's continuing silence, and now that she had discovered she was pregnant—and desperately needing the reassurance of his warmth and love—there didn't seem to be anything she could do but go home to Winterfloods, with her tail firmly between her legs.

'Hello—it is Mrs Link Jameson, isn't it?'

Startled, Polly looked up to see a tall, thin man standing beside her table. Dressed in a pair of old jeans and a battered leather jacket, he seemed a far cry from the usual hotel guest.

'Yes?'

'I've got a letter for you, from your husband,' he said, handing her a grubby envelope.

'Oh, great—thank you!' she smiled up at the man. 'How did you get hold of it...I mean, how is my husband? Is he all right?'

'Oh, sure, he's fine. They're all a bit tired, of course, but otherwise in good shape. And as I fly each day's rushes down to Singapore, he asked me to give you that letter.' He turned to leave. 'I guess I'd better be getting along...'

'Just a moment!' Polly leaped up from the table. 'Are you saying that you fly back and forth, between the location site and Singapore, every day?'

'Yup. Do you want to send a message back to your husband?'

'No—not exactly...' She took a deep breath and gave him a broad, beaming smile. 'Why don't you join me for a cup of coffee, Mr...er...?'

'McGregor. Stan McGregor.'

'Right, Mr McGregor,' Polly said as he sat down and she gave the order to a hovering waiter. 'Now to use that well known American expression—I'd like to make you an offer you can't refuse!'

CHAPTER SEVEN

POLLY hadn't been a farmer for the last three years for nothing, and despite all her problems she thoroughly enjoyed the next half-hour's heavy bargaining session with Stan McGregor.

'I tell you, lady, the way you set about horse-trading, it would make strong men weep. I don't reckon you'd be above stealing the food from a starving man, and that's a fact!' he said with a grin as they shook hands on the deal.

'Oh, come on, Stan—you're no slouch yourself. I should think you could just about retire on what you've screwed out of me,' she laughed.

'Yeah, well...' The smile died on his face. 'It's on the cards that I might lose my job, you know.'

She smiled reassuringly. 'I'm sure you've no need to worry, and if there's any trouble I'll definitely make sure everyone knows that I asked you to fly me up to the camp. So cheer up—and have another cup of coffee, while I cash a cheque and throw a few things into a suitcase.'

'Remember that I've only got room for one small bag,' he warned her.

'I haven't forgotten,' she said, rising from the table and glancing down at her watch. 'It's going to take me some time to get everything sorted out, so I'll meet you in the foyer in about an hour's time.'

The prospect of at last being able to do something positive was exhilarating, and Polly found herself gaily humming a tune as she returned to her suite, quickly throwing some clothes into the small suitcase which she proposed to take with her on the flight up to the camp, where the film company was based.

She knew she was taking a bit of a risk by hitching a lift in Stan McGregor's plane. James wasn't going to be very pleased about her sudden arrival—and that was putting it mildly! However, his own behaviour hadn't been exactly whiter than white, had it? In fact, after talking to Stan, it was quite clear that James must have known soon after arriving at the location site, if not before, that there was a daily shuttle service flying the day's footage to and from the film laboratories in Singapore. It followed, therefore, that he had quite deliberately chosen neither to tell her about the flights, nor to avail himself of the opportunity of coming down to see her during the three weeks she had been stuck in the hotel.

She couldn't even begin to understand why James was treating her with such callousness, and if he objected to her unexpected arrival she wouldn't have the slightest hesitation in pointing out the defects in his own character! However, the last thing she wanted was another quarrel and, if she was prepared to be forgiving about his neglect of his new wife, she was sure that when she told him about the baby, he would immediately understand just how important it had been for her to see him.

It wasn't just the fact that she wanted to tell him about her pregnancy before he went back to

Winterfloods, of course. If she was truly honest, she'd admit that she missed and wanted James so badly that she was prepared to go to any lengths to be with him. Besides that desperate need, nothing else in the world seemed to matter at all.

It was a long, bumpy flight in the light aircraft. After Stan McGregor had called in at the small airport of Kuantan to clear Customs, they finally landed on a makeshift runway in a jungle clearing, and she learned that she still had a river journey ahead of her.

Clambering into the long, slender boat which was set on the river beside the airstrip, Polly was thankful that she had followed Stan's advice to wear something practical. She had been so bored during the last three weeks that, despite not being particularly interested in clothes, she had passed a considerable amount of time by buying herself a completely new wardrobe. All the top designers seemed to have boutiques in Singapore and, despite carrying an expensive label, the green and brown slacks and shirt in a camouflage print were perfect for this sort of terrain.

Sitting in the bows of the boat, she watched while Stan started the outboard motor, allowing her hands to trail idly in the water as they progressed slowly down the river. The jungle loomed heavily on both sides, with its thick wall of greenery reaching to the banks. Many of the trees leaned grotesquely out over the water, and from their branches long, slender vines trailed down to brush against the boat as it passed by. Stan told her that the Malaysian jungles were the oldest on this planet, so old that they made the tropical rain forests of Africa and

South America seem mere adolescents by comparison.

Leaning back in her seat, Polly stared up at the foliage of the jungle trees, arching like the nave of a huge cathedral many hundreds of feet above her. The branches were so dense and interlaced that they provided an almost firm foundation for various species of wildlife, among which she saw some flying lizards and scores of brilliantly feathered birds. She smiled and indicated her pleasure, signalling to Stan over the noise of the outboard engine just how much she was enjoying the trip. It was only when she followed his pointing finger, and saw the patterned markings on the backs of some large tree snakes, lying coiled in the matted vegetation above her head, that she began to lose some of her enthusiasm!

Finally rounding a bend, they saw stretching before them the wide, smooth waters of a huge lake. While Stan cut the motor so that the boat could crawl slowly through a mass of waterlilies barring the entrance to the lake, Polly was entranced by the beauty of their large, deep pink flowers.

'Aren't they lovely? And those leaves are enormous, far larger than anything we have in England,' she enthused. 'I had no idea this was such a vast lake.'

'Yeah, Lake Chini is kinda special,' Stan agreed. 'I was talking to a guy the other day, and he told me that there's supposed to be a lost city somewhere underneath the water. Apparently, it's mentioned in some old Chinese chronicles, and was reckoned to be about the size of Angkor in Cambodia. They also reckon,' he added, 'that there's white crocodiles and a Loch Ness-type of monster somewhere in the lake—but I ain't never seen 'em!'

'I don't think that I'm particularly keen to see any crocodiles!' Polly laughed, leaning back as Stan opened the throttle and they began to cross the wide expanse of water.

She could see why it made a marvellous place to shoot a film, but she privately thought the lake was a bit spooky. The water itself was murky and, from the dark depths, tall, thin branches of mangrove trees, long dead and covered with green slime, protruded eerily through the surface, looking like weird, surrealistic carvings.

Stan brought the small boat to a wooden landing stage. 'Right, this is where you get out,' he said, and, when she had clambered on to the jetty, he handed up her small suitcase. 'I've got to take this lot further on down the river, he added, indicating the heavy portable ice-box containing the large round tins of processed film. 'Mind how you go, now.'

'Thank you so much, Stan. I'm very grateful for all your help,' said Polly as he pointed out a wide path which seemed to lead into dense jungle.

It was the noise of the generators which she heard first of all, the path skirting past them and leading to a neat semicircle of caravans parked some yards away beneath the trees. At the back of the caravans there were various tents and prefabricated buildings, all of which seemed to be completely deserted. Finding one of the caravans had 'Link Jameson' painted on its side, she cautiously opened the door and peered inside. The interior proved to be considerably more spacious than she had expected, with a large double bed at one end, and a seating area with low tables, chairs and a couch at the other.

Since there didn't seem to be anyone around, she decided to investigate further, and was delighted to find a small shower room beside the bed. Wanting to look as pretty as possible for James, and knowing that her pale redhead's skin was ill-suited to the heat, and the muggy, humid atmosphere, she took the opportunity to have a quick wash. There wasn't much she could do about her crumpled jungle suit, but at least the application of some fresh lipstick made her feel in better shape to face a possibly irate husband.

Leaving her case in the caravan, Polly began to explore the camp. Goodness knew where everyone was, but the wide path continued on into the jungle, and was bound to lead somewhere—hopefully towards James and the other members of the film crew.

Half an hour later, hot, tired and bitten all over by mosquitoes, she found herself approaching a large clearing. How she wished she'd listened to James, and had never come near this benighted place, especially since finding those fresh wheel tracks. Why hadn't it occurred to her that the crew were bound to have vehicles of some kind? With motorised transport, they would be able to greatly increase their range. Oh, God—they could be several miles away in the jungle, for all she knew!

Panting from the heat and humidity, she was roused from her deep depression by a familiar sound. If there was one thing she knew about, it was cattle. Somewhere nearby, there was quite obviously a cow—and by the sound of it the animal was in considerable distress. Picking up her tired feet, Polly ran into the clearing and, following the noise, soon came across a small hut with the beast tethered nearby.

'You poor old thing,' she said, running her hand down the pale brown neck of the gaunt and emaciated animal. It was clearly a Brahmin, a variety indigenous to the Far East which she had never seen before, but there was no mistaking the cause of the trouble: the unfortunate cow was long overdue for milking, her udders hot and tender to the touch.

'We'll soon sort that out,' Polly muttered, and after searching through the hut she eventually managed to find a battered, dusty pail. There was no way she could clean the bucket, but this was clearly not the time to be worrying about hygiene, and she returned to squat down beside the cow. Her practised fingers soon began relieving the pressure, the cow ceased to moo quite so piteously, and Polly was just congratulating herself on her long-forgotten and unused expertise in hand-milking, when a vehicle drove into the clearing.

Unable to turn her head, which was buried in the cow's flank, she could only hear the loud bang of a car door, and heavy footsteps approaching as a rough, American voice shouted, 'Hey, you guy— what in the hell do you think you're doing?'

'I'm not a guy—and what does it look as if I'm doing?' she retorted.

'You're not supposed to be milking that cow!'

'Well, that's just too bad,' Polly snapped. 'This animal was... *Leave me alone!*' she cried as the man grabbed her arm and jerked her away from the cow.

'Now look what you've done,' she shouted in disgust as the pail tipped over and the milk ran out over the dusty ground.

'It's nothing to what *you've* done—you stupid broad!' the large, fat man growled, before swearing violently as she kicked him hard in the shins, forcing him to let go of her arm. 'What ya do that for?' he groaned, hopping about in pain as he clutched his leg.

'I don't like being grabbed by strange men. And I'll do it again if you so much as lay a finger on me—so watch out!' she warned.

'You're the one who's going to have to watch out. Donald's going to be real mad when he finds out what you've done. Oh yes, you're in deep trouble, lady,' the fat man said, with obvious relish. 'Now, get in the jeep, and start saying your prayers,' he added, pointing towards the vehicle parked nearby.

Polly thought quickly. Donald Buckley was the director of the movie, and at least by going with this obnoxious man she would be able to find the rest of the film crew—and James. Giving the American a scathing look, she stalked over to the jeep and clambered aboard.

'Who in the hell are you, anyway?' the man asked as he drove out of the clearing.

'I'm Link Jameson's wife,' she said curtly.

The man looked at her with astonishment. 'Jesus! Poor ol' Link—he must have a hell of a life with you, lady!'

'When I want to know your opinion, I'll ask for it,' she snapped, her irritation increasing when he didn't apologise for being so impertinent, but continued to mutter, 'Poor ol' Link...' several times under his breath.

The jeep wound its way through the jungle, coming at last to a halt by a narrow creek at the edge of the lake, where a large group of people were milling around a makeshift tent, munching sandwiches and drinking from plastic cups.

'Come along,' the fat man said, leading the way towards the tent. 'I wouldn't miss this for the world!'

The director, Donald Buckley, was looking somewhat harassed as her captor pulled him to one side to relate the episode with the cow. Polly, for her part, hardly noticed—she was much too busy scanning the faces of the crowd for a sight of James. Not seeing him, she went over to a girl carrying a clipboard in one hand, and a large stop-watch in the other.

'Have you seen James? I mean, is Link Jameson anywhere about?'

'Nope, sorry,' the girl replied quickly, before turning to shout at a group of men, 'Come on, boys—let's get the rehearsal started. Take up your places from the last take.'

'Don't you have *any* idea where Link could be?' Polly asked anxiously.

'Sure I do. He went off down the river with the second unit for some location shots, and won't be back till late tonight. Now, if you don't mind,' the girl added caustically, 'I've got some work to do. Why don't you...'

'What's this I hear about the cow?' Donald's angry voice cut across whatever the girl may have been about to say, and Polly turned quickly to face him.

'I don't know what all the fuss is about,' she shrugged. 'The cow just needed milking, that's all.'

'I *know* the cow hadn't been milked—that was the whole point of the exercise,' Donald grated, waving away the girl with the clipboard. 'We needed the animal to be bellowing, for the next take. And now, thanks to your meddling, we're going to have to put that scene off until tomorrow.'

'Rescuing an animal in pain is not meddling!' she retorted angrily. 'And it's disgraceful to use or treat a cow like that—you should be ashamed of yourself. As for what the animal welfare people would say...'

'This is Malaysia, Mrs Jameson—not downtown New York!' the director ground out bitterly. 'And I don't need uppity females, like you, disrupting my schedule.'

Polly was just about to give Donald Buckley her full, frank views on film directors who tortured helpless animals, when she was distracted by the sound of a gunshot. Spinning around, she saw that the crowd of people had dispersed, leaving only a man rapidly firing a rifle into the water. Looking across the creek, she could see a young girl who looked about twelve years of age, splashing and shouting as she pointed to a long, grey, vicious-looking crocodile. Another man was swimming frantically towards her, but he obviously had some way to go and was unlikely to reach the girl in time.

Summing up the situation at a glance, and noting that the man with the rifle seemed incapable of hitting anything, since his shots were well wide of the crocodile, she leaped forward and seized the weapon from his hand. With a smooth movement, she raised the gun, letting off two quick shots into the head of the fearsome reptile.

The overwhelming reaction—and chaos—which resulted from her accurate marksmanship, was not at all what she expected.

The man from whom she had seized the gun was looking at her with an expression of stunned amazement, while the girl and the man in the water began shouting to each other in bewilderment—as was practically every other member of the film crew, who were pouring in from all sides. It wasn't until Donald Buckley, trembling with fury, came rushing up to her side, that she had some inkling of the truth.

'You damn stupid woman!' he thundered, pointing to the water, where someone was lifting up the crocodile. As Polly gazed down, she could see a large, gaping hole in the head, from which air was fast escaping. Even as she watched, what had been a rigid form began to crumple up, and she saw that the 'crocodile' was nothing more than an inflatable, plastic imitation of the real thing!

'Oh, God—I'm sorry,' she muttered, trying not to giggle at the ridiculous sight.

'*You're sorry?* That croc cost a fortune back in the States—so where in the hell do you think I'm going to get another one of those for the final shot?' the director shouted, almost tearing his hair in rage. 'Get her out of here—quickly, before she does any more damage!' he added furiously, instructing a driver to take Polly back to the camp and not, under pain of death, to let her anywhere near the set again.

She didn't seem to be able to do *anything* right, Polly told herself later that night. Lying huddled up on the couch as she waited for James's return to the camp, she reflected gloomily that her first foray into the film world had been a complete disaster. She still had no regrets about saving the cow from any further pain. To have used an animal in that way was nothing short of disgraceful. In fact, those sort of artificial, illusionary tricks—who could have possibly guessed that the crocodile was a fake?—were simply light years away from her prosaic life on a farm. She felt totally out of place in her new husband's world, and she very much feared that she never would understand it. Her glum thoughts were interrupted as the door of the caravan opened and James staggered in, his tall figure covered in filthy rags.

'Darling!' She leaped up from the couch and went over to put her arms around me.

'Don't touch me,' he said quickly as he evaded her hands. 'I'm covered in stinking mud and dirty water.'

'Oh, James, I hope you don't mind ... you don't think ...'

'Sweetheart—I'm too damn tired to mind or think anything,' he said wearily. 'Frankly, it's been a hell of a day and I'm exhausted. All I want is a hot shower and a long sleep,' he added with a tired smile as he slowly made his way towards the other end of the caravan.

So much for the romantic reunion! Polly thought disconsolately some time later, gazing over at James's comatose figure. He had returned from the shower, given her a brief wave of his hand before dropping down on to the bed, and falling asleep almost before his head hit the pillows. The only consolation was that he hadn't bawled her out over the day's disasters. But he would undoubtedly do so when he woke up, she realised as she went over to lie down beside him. The thought of what he was likely to say or do tomorrow kept her awake for a long time, and it wasn't until the early hours of the morning that she fell into a restless sleep.

When she awoke, it was to find the sun pouring in through the windows, and the caravan deserted. Oh, lord—she'd overslept and missed the opportunity for a long talk with James. Hurrying into her clothes, she left the caravan and ran along the path which led to the creek. She remembered Donald's words about barring her from the set, and resolved to keep well out of sight until she could find James. Finally, rounding a sharp bend, she realised that she had reached the set, which was set further up the creek where the water narrowed into a thin channel between high banks. And, unlike yesterday's rehearsal, it looked as if they really were filming this time.

After the dim, green light of the jungle path it was some moments before her eyes were able to adjust to the brilliant sodium light from the arc lamps, used to reinforce the morning sun. All she could really see were the backs of actors and crew members standing or sitting beneath some large, brightly coloured umbrellas positioned on the top of the bank, and obviously being used to shade the cameras and other various pieces of film apparatus. Edging around a large green tent, where two actors were having mud artistically splashed on to their bodies, she dodged quickly back as she saw Donald a few feet away, giving instructions to the cameramen. Taking cover behind a tree hanging over the bank, Polly cautiously peered around the trunk to stare down at the wide sandbanks on either side of the brown, muddy water.

For someone not used to a film unit, it was a confusing and chaotic sight. Various members of the crew appeared to be moving slowly and aimlessly around, although as she watched it became apparent that it was the lighting of the set which was causing problems. Eventually, they became galvanised into action, feverishly brushing the soft sand to obliterate their footprints as Donald Buckley called for silence.

'OK,' he said through a megaphone, his disembodied voice echoing eerily in the still, quiet air. 'Stand by for Scene 532, Take Seven. And, for God's sake, let's get this one in the can!'

As a young man darted forward with a clapperboard, Polly discovered there were two cameras in use, one on each side of the creek, and both of them seemed to be filming at the same time. But what? The scene below appeared to be totally deserted. She leant forward, and it was only then that she saw a man and a woman thrashing and fighting their way through the water towards her. The man was filthy dirty, his magnificent physique barely covered by tattered rags and the waist-high water as he struggled to retain hold of the woman, who was clearly trying to escape his clutches. With a loud cry, she broke free and made a dash for the sandbank beneath where Polly was standing. The woman had almost reached dry land, when the man gave a final spurt and threw himself on top of her, both of them falling down to lie half-in and half-out of the water. There was a long pause as they stared silently at each other, before he gave a deep groan and ripped away the thin cotton sarong clinging to her wet body.

Polly had been so caught up in the action that it was some moments before she began to comprehend the awful truth. It was no actor in a drama, but James—*her husband!*—who was now moving his hands slowly and deliberately over the woman's naked breasts. And—and it wasn't just a simple native woman down there, it...*it was Melody Grant!*

Paralysed with shock, she was unable to tear her horrified eyes away from the two lovers, now panting and writhing in the throes of a torrid, passionate scene of unbridled lust. As James lowered his head towards the hard peaks of Melody's ripe, swollen breasts, something seemed to snap in Polly's brain. With a loud cry of anguish, she rushed forward, completely forgetting where she was as she stepped out into space, tumbling head over heels down on to the sandbank, six feet below.

'...And not content with making a fool of yourself—an aim in which you succeeded brilliantly, I may add!—it now seems that you've also managed to break poor Melody's ankle. Well done, Polly!' James grated savagely as he re-entered the caravan.

Sitting huddled in the corner, her shivering wet body wrapped in a rough blanket, Polly closed her eyes as James paced furiously up and down the

confined space. It was over two hours since she had
made her completely unscheduled appearance in
Scene 532, Take Seven, of *None But the Brave*.
Unfortunately, she didn't remember anything of her
rapid descent from the high bank. It was only when
she came back to full consciousness, as she was
being carried into the caravan, that she realised what
had happened. And, apart from a few minutes just
now, when he had left her to discover the latest
news about Melody's injury, James had spent the
last two hours telling her exactly what he thought
of her conduct—both yesterday and today—and he
certainly hadn't restrained either his words or his
temper.

'Quite apart from the fact that Melody will
probably sue you for well over a million dollars—
and I wouldn't blame her for one minute if she
did!—do you have any idea of how much damage
you've caused to this film? Lord knows when we're
going to be able to get back on schedule, if at all.
And when the studio management learn that it's all
my wife's fault, any court case instituted by Donald
for lost time, or Melody for her injury, will look
like peanuts compared to the law suit they're likely
to bring against me. I'll be damn lucky if I come
out of this fiasco with the shirt still on my back!'
he thundered angrily.

'I'm very... very s-sorry,' she whispered.

'I should damn well think you are! And I haven't
mentioned my own career yet, have I?' he added
bitterly. 'It's only a small matter compared to the
rest of the mayhem you've caused, of course, but
there's no doubt that now—thanks to my *darling*
wife making such an ass of herself—I'm going to

be the laughing stock of the industry for years to come. Thanks a bunch, sweetheart!'

'I never meant...I never thought...'

James gave a harsh, cruel laugh. 'Sure, you didn't. In fact, I'd be surprised if you've ever thought about anyone else in the whole of your life. You certainly didn't give a hoot in hell about me!'

'That—that's totally untrue and unfair!' she cried.

'Oh, yeah? Right from the moment we arrived in Singapore, our relationship took a sharp nose-dive, and it's continued downhill all the way. First, there was all that nonsense about my so-called relationship with Melody. I told you I wasn't in the slightest bit interested, but you clearly didn't believe a word I said. Oh, no—you knew better!'

He thrust his hands roughly through his dark hair. 'And then there was your obsession about coming up here to the location site. Why should you bother to listen to my advice? You were quite convinced that I was just trying to be difficult, and it certainly never occurred to you that, since I've been in this business for a number of years, I might just happen to know what I was talking about. You were quite determined to get yourself up here, by hook or by crook,' he continued, his voice thick with fury. 'And you sure as hell succeeded! My God—I nearly died when I looked up and saw you falling down towards me like a bomb out of the sky. It was just Melody's bad luck that she hadn't time to avoid part of that tree you brought down with you, wasn't it? And as for you?' He gave a bitter, contemptuous laugh. 'The good Lord clearly looks after fools and idiots, because you haven't got even one scratch on your body!'

Polly clasped her arms about her legs, burying her face against her shivering knees. 'I—I've told you that I'm desperately sorry that I've caused all this trouble,' she whispered helplessly. 'I'll apologise to Melody just as soon as I can, and—and of course I will pay her doctor's bills, and for any damage to her career.'

'That sounds all very fine and noble,' he retorted. 'However, I don't think you have any idea of the astronomical sums awarded in the American courts. It's more than likely that you'll probably have to sell your precious farm to raise the money,' he added cruelly. 'And, talking of hard cash, I hope Stan McGregor feels he's got his money's worth from you, because I hear he's been sacked, and hasn't a hope in hell of ever getting another job with an American film company.'

'Oh, n-no!' she moaned.

'Oh, yes, I'm afraid so,' he said flatly. 'And for goodness' sake, stop shivering as though I'm going to beat you up any minute. I've never hit a woman in my life—although, God knows, I've been sorely tempted to thrash the living daylights out of you this afternoon!'

'I c-can't. It's the air-conditioning. I'm so c-cold,' she stuttered, her teeth chattering loudly in her head.

James went over to press down a switch, before throwing himself down into a cane chair, and giving a heavy sigh. 'There's no point in my going on, is there?' he said bleakly. 'It's probably all my fault, anyway. I never should have made the mistake of getting married and bringing you out here with me.'

'Please don't...don't say that,' she moaned, gasping with pain as if she'd just been stabbed in the heart. 'I love you, I...'

'Do you, Polly?'

She moistened her dry lips with the tip of her tongue, feeling sick with apprehension and rising panic as she stared at the hard, implacably grim expression on his face. 'You know that I do. That when we...when we made love, you and I...' Her face burned. 'Oh, James—you know very well...'

'That our sex life was good?' he retorted, almost contemptuously. 'Sure it was. But outside the bedroom—zilch! As far as our marriage is concerned, it seems to me that I've been the one to make all the concessions. We were going to live in your house, on your farm, right? You were going to keep on doing what you'd always done, with very little disturbance from me, right? The only thing I asked of you—that I should have some authority in our own home—practically provoked World War Three, right? Even my wish to keep you well away from the bitchy film world, and the boring, uncomfortably hard and tedious life here on location—was something that you totally disregarded, *right*? In fact, during the whole of our brief, married life, it's been a case of what *you* wanted—and to hell with anyone else's feelings!'

'No! No, that's not true...' she cried, his cruel words pounding through her aching head like a sledge-hammer. And then she suddenly realised that she hadn't told him about the baby. 'You don't understand. The reason I'm here is because I had to see you...'

'Fine—so you've seen me.' His hard voice cut ruthlessly across her words. 'And I hope you feel it's been worth it,' he added as he rose from the chair. 'To put it very crudely: you may be great in bed, sweetheart, but in every other facet of our marriage you've clearly demonstrated that you aren't capable of loving anyone other than yourself.'

'But you have to listen to me!' she wailed.

'I don't *have* to do anything,' he said coldly, walking over to the door of the caravan. 'Except arrange for your transport out of here as quickly as possible. It's obvious that the sooner you go back to your farm, and your own way of life, the better.'

'*James! Don't go!*' she cried, struggling to escape from the heavy folds of the large blanket. But her urgent plea fell on deaf ears as he slammed the door firmly behind his departing figure.

Polly was in the large barn, checking the stocks of winter feed and hay, when through the large open doors she saw a white Range Rover enter the farmyard. She'd been expecting this, of course. Ever since Elsie had come upon her unexpectedly yesterday, and caught her in the midst of a heavy bout of morning sickness, she had known that she wasn't going to be able to keep her pregnancy a secret much longer. Even while she'd been swearing the old housekeeper to silence, she'd realised that it was probably a waste of time. However hard she tried, Elsie would never have been able to keep that sort of information to herself, and the first person she was bound to tell would undoubtedly have been her sister, Mrs Renshaw, the housekeeper up at Eastdale Hall. With a heavy sigh, Polly put her notebook into the pocket of her dungarees, and walked out into the yard to greet her stepmother.

'Darling—why didn't you tell me?' Alicia smiled happily as she clambered down from the vehicle in an ungainly fashion, and came over to put her arms about Polly's stiff figure. 'I was so excited to hear the news from Elsie that I simply had to come down here, straight away. Isn't it wonderful—the two of us having babies together?'

'Just wonderful,' Polly echoed heavily, staring dully at the beautiful woman who was only four years older than herself. Alicia had never been anything less than lovely, of course, but now there was an extra sparkle in her wide blue eyes, an added softness to the delicate peaches and cream complexion, surrounded by a cloud of ash-blonde hair which was caught into a chignon at the nape of her slender neck. Polly loved her stepmother very much, but she knew that her own thin, strained features must look grotesque when compared to Alicia's radiant beauty. She gave a sigh and said, 'Would you like a cup of tea?'

'Mmm, lovely,' Alicia murmured as they made their way into the house. 'But why on earth didn't you tell me?' she continued, sitting down on a chair in the kitchen. 'You've been back here at Winterfloods for almost three weeks, and yet you've never said a word. What does James think? He must be thrilled to bits, of course, and I expect he wants a boy. Giles seems to be obsessed with the idea of having a son and heir,' she laughed. 'I've given up trying to point out that there's an equal chance that I might have a girl!'

'Milk and sugar?'

'No sugar, I'm trying to watch my weight,' Alicia said, looking ruefully down at her stomach. 'Honestly, I'm not yet quite five months' pregnant, and I'm already looking like a hot-air balloon! So tell me,' she added, sipping her tea, 'when's your baby due?'

Polly shrugged. 'I haven't a clue.'

'Well, what does the doctor say?'

'I don't know. I haven't been to see a doctor yet,' Polly answered glumly.

'But, darling, you must go and see someone as soon as possible. It's terribly important to have good ante-natal care,' Alicia said, looking anxiously at her stepdaughter, who seemed quite extraordinarily uninterested in the fact that she was expecting a baby. 'I don't want to nag, but I'm sure that if James were here he'd agree with me.'

There was a long silence as Polly stared down into her cup. 'It—it's all a bit complicated,' she said at last. 'The plain fact is——' she raised her green eyes to meet Alicia's puzzled frown '—James doesn't know I'm pregnant. And I don't know if I'm still married to him or not.'

'*What?*' Alicia gasped. 'You don't mean...you're not telling me that there was something wrong with the wedding service? I—well, I'd never have believed that the Rector would have...'

Polly gave a bark of harsh laughter. 'You've got quite the wrong end of the stick, I'm afraid,' she said grimly. 'There's nothing technically wrong with my marriage—nothing, other than the fact that I rather think my husband has left me. Or I've left him. I'm not entirely sure of the protocol as far as divorce is concerned,' she added wearily.

'Oh, no—surely not?' Alicia looked at her in consternation. 'Elsie told me that you were both so very much in love. I thought . . . when you returned from Malaysia, I understood that James would be joining you at the farm just as soon as his filming was finished.'

Polly shrugged unhappily. 'I had to say something, didn't I? I—I was too proud . . . I simply couldn't face having to tell everyone the truth,' she muttered huskily, rising from her chair and going over to stare blindly out of the window. 'I suppose I was still hoping and praying that he . . .' Her voice trailed away as she swallowed hard against the lump in her throat.

'Oh—Polly!' Alicia cried, jumping up and going over to put her arms tightly about the girl's trembling figure. 'It's going to be all right, darling,' she murmured softly as Polly put her head against her shoulder and burst into tears. 'I'm here now. I'll look after you,' she said, her voice warm and soothing as she gently stroked her stepdaughter's shaking body.

'I'm s-sorry,' Polly muttered at last, when her storm of weeping had abated. 'I hate people who are always s-snivelling,' she moaned, hunting frantically for a handkerchief.

'I should think a good cry was just what you needed,' Alicia said sympathetically. 'Now, let's sit down and have another cup of tea, and you can tell me about it. I'm sure your problems aren't half

as bad as you think they are,' she added, handing
Polly some tissues. 'I'm told that being pregnant
can make some people very over-emotional, and I
know that I've been over-reacting to a number of
situations which normally wouldn't worry me at all.'

'I only wish I *was* over-reacting or being over-
emotional,' Polly sniffed miserably, fiercely blowing
her nose before sitting down and giving her
stepmother a detailed account of her brief marriage.

'And...and after James had slammed out of the
caravan, he arranged for me to be taken up to the
rather primitive resthouse, hired by the film
company at Kuala Tahan, and I didn't see or hear
anything of him for the next three days. In fact,'
she added as fresh tears began trickling down her
cheeks, 'the only person who spoke to me, or was
even half-way decent, was the film company's resi-
dent doctor—and only because I seemed to have
caught a feverish cold, and there was a question as
to whether I was well enough to fly back to
England,' she sniffed. 'And the car journey to a
small, local airport was the last time I saw James.'

'Surely that must have given you an opportunity
to talk things over, and for you to tell him about
the baby?'

Polly shook her head. 'No—we hardly ex-
changed a word.'

'But that's terrible! I've never heard of anything
so disgraceful!' Alicia exclaimed, her cheeks pink
with indignation. 'How could your husband possibly treat you like that? He sounds horribly cruel
and unkind!'

'No—no, he's not like that at all.' Polly rubbed her red, swollen eyes. 'That's the problem, you see.'

'Darling, I'm sorry, but I really *don't* see.' Alicia gazed at her stepdaughter with a puzzled frown. 'I mean, of course I can see you've got a lot of problems, but they aren't your fault...'

'Yes, they are!' Polly cried. 'I was... well, I was shocked and hurt and... and really angry when he said all those horrid things, and accused me of being totally selfish. But, since I've been back here at the farm, I've had all these days and weeks to do nothing but think, and... and the really awful, ghastly thing is—*I've realised that he's absolutely right!*' she wailed, burying her head in her hands, her body shaking and convulsed by sobs.

'Oh, darling, you mustn't cry like this,' Alicia murmured, putting her arm about the girl's thin shoulders.

'You see...' Polly hiccuped and grabbed some more tissues. 'I—I really do love James with all my heart, but we... well, I realise now that he was right when he said I was "one tough lady". I always did expect to get my own way in everything, and... and I didn't really think about anyone else at all. I broke that horrid actress's ankle, and the poor pilot, Stan McGregor, was sacked from his job, all because I was determined to get my own selfish way.' She blew her nose fiercely. 'And the truth is that James did apologise for having lost his temper, and he was trying to be nice and kind on the way to the airport, but I was so ill with morning sickness, and so... so furiously angry with him, that—— Oh, Alicia!' she almost howled with pain. 'I told him that I never wanted to see him again, and the sooner we got a divorce, the better!'

CHAPTER EIGHT

'LOVE hurts . . . Love scars . . .'

It certainly does, Polly thought miserably, as the lyrical strains of the sad love-song filled her bedroom. With a sigh, she leaned forwards and frowned at her reflection in the dressing-table mirror. She was going to have to do something about those dark shadows beneath her eyes. Alicia had been very firm on the telephone this morning.

'You're looking positively haggard these days, Polly. You've got to pull yourself together,' she had said briskly, before issuing her invitation for dinner tonight. Riding roughshod over her stepdaughter's attempt to refuse what was clearly a royal command, she had declared, 'It's no good trying to tell me that you have to see to the cows—Giles says it will be a good week before they start calving. So we'll see you at eight. And, for goodness' sake, try and wear a decent dress for once,' she added, putting down the phone before Polly could argue any further.

Alicia meant well, of course, but it looked as if breaking down and pouring out all her woes to her stepmother the other day had been a grave mistake. Not only was Alicia determined to forcibly drag her from her melancholy, dejected state, but she'd also clearly had a word with both her husband, Giles, and Elsie. Polly had been able to cope with the housekeeper's warm, heavy sympathy a lot more easily than with Giles's embarrassment at having been prodded into giving a bracing talk to his stepdaughter.

'Relax, Giles,' she had said, after he had muttered a few optimistic clichés. 'There's nothing wrong with me that being left alone to sort out my own problems won't cure. And if you want to give me some good advice,' she had added with a wintery smile, 'I'd be grateful if you'd come and have a look at one of the young heifers. She's not looking too good, and I'd like to hear your opinion.'

It was only after they had inspected the animal, and he was about to leave, that Giles had returned to the subject. 'Don't make the same mistake as Alicia and myself,' he had said quietly, leaning his tall figure casually against the open door of the Range Rover. 'We were both so stiff with pride, each of us so determined not to be the first one to admit how much we loved each other . . .' He sighed heavily, the lines deepening in his arrogant, handsome face. 'We wasted so many years—long, precious years which have now gone for ever. Don't follow our stupid example, Polly. No amount of pride or face-saving is worth that sort of foolish stubbornness.'

'Love is like a fire . . . it burns so hot . . .' Polly sighed, getting up to switch off the stereo. She must stop wallowing in misery like this. Sitting around listening to sad love-songs wasn't going to achieve anything, and it certainly wasn't going to bring James back. After listening to Giles's good advice, she had taken her courage in both hands and written a long letter to James. The problem had been where to send it. In the end, she had despatched it off to the headquarters of the film company in Hollywood, but even if it was delivered to the right place it would probably be regarded as just another fan letter. Polly could feel the familiar weight of dark, heavy depression settling on her shoulders as she realised that, despite the many hours she'd spent over its composition, the chances of James actually reading her letter were very slim indeed. But at least she'd conquered her pride and made the effort, just as she was forcing herself to join the dinner party tonight.

Turning to leave the room, she gave herself a final inspection in the mirror. She hoped that Alicia, who was always nagging her about her total lack of interest in high fashion, would be suitably impressed by the horrendously expensive, midnight-blue silk dress she had bought in Singapore. Looking at the shimmering material, which emphasized the slender curves of her body, she found it difficult to believe that she really was pregnant, although all the doctor's tests had definitely confirmed that she was. It had been a bit embarrassing to have to go and see Ray Martin about the baby, but he had been really very sweet and reassuring. Not only did he already know about her marriage, having seen the Press photographs taken at the time of her wedding, but she was relieved when he made a point of telling her that he was now dating one of the nurses in the surgery.

Maybe he and his new girlfriend will be here tonight, Polly thought as she drew her red Ferrari to a halt outside the portico of Eastdale Hall. But, after greeting the butler, and following him as he led her into the drawing-room to be announced, she found that the other guests were all complete strangers.

Sipping her glass of sherry, she was making idle conversation with an industrialist from the Midlands, and privately thinking how lucky it was that Alicia liked the starchy, formal way of life that went with being the local squire's wife—a fate worse than death as far as she was concerned—when the butler appeared once more in the doorway.

He gave a slight cough to attract his mistress's attention, and Alicia came forward with a polite smile as he announced in ringing accents, 'Mr James Linklater.'

Polly had heard of the expression, 'to go hot and cold all over', and that seemed to be a fair description of the tremors—at first blazing hot and then freezing cold—which flared and raged through her trembling body.

James? Here at Eastdale Hall? She closed her eyes for a moment as she fought to remain standing upright, her legs shaking as if they were made of jelly. Yes, it really was James walking into the room, looking impossibly handsome in a formal dinner suit, the white silk shirt emphasising his deeply tanned features. And talk about being 'cool'! The damn man was looking perfectly at ease and totally relaxed—as if he hadn't a care in the world!

Not so his hostess. If she, herself, hadn't been so stunned with shock, Polly might have laughed at the way Alicia's smile of welcome remained fixed, as if her facial muscles had suddenly become paralysed, while her wide blue eyes registered horrified embarrassment. Unfortunately, there was nothing she could do to help her stepmother. She was much

too preoccupied in trying to remain upright, not
daring to let go of the tall chair beside her, to which
she was now clinging for dear life.

In fact, it was solely thanks to Giles that they
managed to brush through the first few awkward
moments. You could say what you liked about the
upper classes—and she had said quite a few hard
things in her time—but there was no doubt that all
that *noblesse oblige* and centuries of 'rising to the
occasion', certainly paid off in times of dire ex-
tremity. She'd never been so proud of anyone as
she was of the way Giles immediately took charge
of the potentially explosive situation.

'My dear fellow,' he drawled, moving smoothly
forward to shake James's hand. 'How nice to see
you! Now, let's see, who haven't you met? Ah, yes,
you must come and have a talk with our local
Member of Parliament. He's about to make a fact-
finding mission to Los Angeles, and I'm sure you'll
be able to give him a lot of valuable information,'
he added, adroitly steering James away from the
door, and Polly's stunned, trembling figure.

'What's he doing here?' Alicia hissed out of the
corner of her mouth.

'How would I know?' Polly groaned helplessly,
unable to tear her eyes away from the tall,
handsome figure of her husband. However, thanks
to Giles's swift interception, she had a few minutes
in which to pull her shattered senses together, before
James finished talking to the garrulous MP, and
began making his way over to where Polly was
mentally, if not physically, holding Alicia's hand.

'I'm sorry I'm late, sweetheart,' he said, giving
Polly a lazy, bland smile, before turning his at-

tention—and his brilliant blue eyes—on to his hostess.

Honestly, he really was the living end! Still feeling shattered by his unexpected appearance, she found herself trapped and forced to stand helplessly by as James deliberately set out to charm her stepmother. It was almost unbelievable, but in what appeared to be the twinkling of an eye he was managing to change Alicia's obvious hostility into what Polly could only think of as revolting, simpering adoration.

'He's *so* charming, and quite fantastically good-looking!' Alicia whispered as James went to fetch her a glass of white wine.

'Don't be fooled. He's only acting, for God's sake!' Polly hissed. 'And if you dare to tell him about the baby—I'll kill you! Or Giles will, especially if you keep on flirting with James like that,' she ground out through clenched teeth.

But Giles, who was normally a very jealous husband, seemed strangely uninterested in his wife's quite blatant flirtation with James, and, after they had adjourned to the dining-room, he skilfully drew from James some amusing stories and anecdotes about his life in the movies. In fact, Polly thought gloomily, her husband was the hit of the dinner party, with everyone thrilled to have a genuine, real live film star in their midst, and it was only his own wife to whom he said hardly a word.

Sitting silently beside him through what seemed to be the longest, most interminable meal she could ever remember, she was at first deeply annoyed and then increasingly angry at the way he was practically ignoring her existence. If he wasn't interested in her, what on earth was he doing here in Shropshire? And, if he *had* come all this way to see her, he certainly had a damn fine way of showing it!

At last the dinner party drew to a close. Wild fantasies, such as dashing upstairs and locking herself into one of the bedrooms of Eastdale Hall, had flitted through Polly's tired brain, but James gave her no opportunity for escape. As soon as they rose from the table he made their excuses, thanked Giles and Alicia for a delicious dinner and, clasping her arm, led her silently down the flight of stone steps to where she had parked the Ferrari, equally silently handing her into the passenger seat.

God—what an evening! Leaning back against the headrest, Polly closed her eyes and gave a sigh of utter weariness. She honestly couldn't remember ever feeling so mentally worn out. From the moment when James had suddenly materialised like the demon king in a pantomime—and the only feature missing from his shocking, unexpected appearance had been the traditional puff of green smoke!—the evening had been one of the most exhausting experiences of her life.

'Wake up, Polly!'

'What?' She turned her dazed eyes towards the man now sitting in the car beside her.

'Don't go off to sleep before you give me the car keys,' he said, his voice heavy with amusement. 'I can't get us home without them.'

'Oh, yes—um—sorry...' she mumbled, her hands trembling so much that it took her a moment or two before she managed to find them in a corner of her bag. And the touch of his warm hand, as he took them from her shaking fingers, did nothing to improve her equilibrium.

'Home', he'd said. Did he really mean it, or was it just an American euphemism? The beastly man hadn't given a thing away during dinner, and the way he had quite clearly set out to charm and flirt with Alicia had been nothing short of disgusting!

By the time James drove the car into the farmyard, Polly was in such a state of nervous tension that she could hardly speak. And it seemed to take the most enormous effort before she was able to say the few simple words, 'Would you like a cup of coffee?'

'Hmm, that would be very nice,' he replied smoothly, getting out to come around and open her door. She looked up into his face, illuminated by the light outside the hay barn. She could have sworn... for almost a second, it had sounded as if he was laughing at her, but his face was devoid of all expression, and she needed all her concentration to get herself out of the car and into the house. It was either nerves, or all those glasses of wine she had been unhappily tipping down her throat during dinner, but her legs felt as if they were made of cotton wool.

Polly took as much time as she could about filling the kettle, putting it on the stove and getting out the cups and saucers from the kitchen cupboard. James seemed quite content, sitting on one of the kitchen chairs and quietly smoking one of his cheroots, but she found the lack of conversation acutely oppressive, and eventually the strained silence became too much for her to bear. She hadn't a clue what to say, but if she didn't think of some-

thing fairly quickly she knew that she was going to
break down into floods of tears, and beg James to
stay with her for ever. And that could be the
greatest, and most humiliating, mistake of her life.
For all she knew, he might have just come back to
fetch a few of his clothes which were still upstairs,
or the pile of his books in the sitting-room.

'That was a very—er—very nice meal, wasn't it?'
she said at last.

'Hmm, very nice,' he agreed smoothly.

She waited for him to say something else but,
when he remained obstinately silent, she turned
away and scowled down at the kettle which was,
equally obstinately, refusing to come to the boil.

'I—I wondered what . . . well, what you're doing
here?' she muttered, throwing him a quick,
sideways glance.

He raised a dark eyebrow in surprise. 'What an
extraordinary question. Why shouldn't I be here?
It's my home, isn't it?'

'Well, I thought . . .'

'Hmm?'

'I—I thought you wouldn't . . . well, you might
not want to see me again,' she said, holding her
breath and saying a fervent prayer.

'Now, I wonder why you should think that?' he
murmured blandly.

Oh, God—for two pins, she'd hit the horrid man!
He wasn't giving her any help, and it must be
glaringly obvious—even to a blind man—exactly
what she was trying to say. James must think her
a complete idiot if he thought she didn't know what
he was up to. He was clearly determined to get his
pound of flesh, and there wasn't a damn thing she

could do about it—not if she loved and needed him. *And, oh, yes, she did—quite desperately!*

'Look, James, you can stop playing games,' she said at last, giving him a wobbly, almost tearful smile. 'Knowing me, I'll probably kick your shins in later, but right now...' She paused and took a deep, shaky breath. 'I suppose I'd better start by saying that you were quite right to accuse me of being supremely selfish. I was. I was totally absorbed by what I wanted to do, and it simply never occurred to me to consider other peoples' wishes and desires. Or if it did,' she added, 'I would only think about them within the context of how I could best get my own way. I—I have seen the light now, and I am trying to mend my ways. But, if I'm going to be truly honest,' she gave him a shaky, crooked grin, 'I've still got a long way to go. I'm afraid that I'm not exactly the humble type.'

'Well, that's a mercy!' James gave a low, sardonic laugh. 'I don't think I could stand you in the role of the meek, little wife—and it would be clearly out of character, in any case.'

'All right, all right—there's no need to rub it in!' she snapped angrily.

'Careful!' he warned. 'You were doing splendidly; it would be a shame to spoil it now.'

Polly groaned. 'Oh, James—please don't be so unkind. Have I really got to go through with this?'

'They say that confession is good for the soul,' he murmured.

'They are lying!' she assured him grimly. 'Oh, all right,' she sighed as he continued to gaze at her with an expression of bland interest on his handsome face, 'I freely admit that I should have listened to your advice. You knew what you were talking about, and I was an idiot to think, as far as the film world is concerned, that I knew better. What else...?' she frowned, and then flushed as she remembered her behaviour when she had last seen him. 'I—I don't want a divorce. I never wanted one, and I don't know what got into me on that awful trip to the airport, for the flight to Kuala Lumpur. I was a perfect bitch.' She looked at him sorrowfully. 'In fact, I was just as bad as Melody— well, worse really,' she added reflectively, 'because she can't really help being foul and...'

Her voice trailed away as he threw back his head and roared with laughter. 'Polly—you're priceless!' he said, rising to his feet and coming over to take her into his arms. 'I love you—and I've missed you like hell, sweetheart,' he murmured before possessing her mouth in a kiss of heart-stopping warmth and tenderness. 'And it wasn't all your fault,' he said softly, crushing her trembling figure in a tight embrace. 'Not only did I lose my temper as I've never done before—and I hope to God I never do again—but I was unreasonably hard on you. I should never have dragged you into that crazy, bitchy world with so little preparation. So I guess it's my turn to say I'm also very sorry, and I'll try to be a better husband in future.' He stared down into her green eyes. 'That's if you still want to stay married to me?'

'Now who's being humble?' She gave a tearful gurgle of laughter, which turned into a squeal as he swept her up in his arms. 'What do you think you're doing?' she demanded as he kicked open the kitchen door and moved across the hall towards the staircase.

'Oh, come on, sweetheart,' he drawled mockingly. 'We may have had plenty of problems, but if I recall the matter correctly—and you can bet your bottom dollar that I do—making love wasn't one of them!'

'Well, if you're going to stay married to me, you'll have to stop kicking in that kitchen door,' she grumbled happily as he tossed her down on to the bed.

James laughed. 'The answer's simple: all we have to do is to take the damn door off its hinges, which will mean that I can get you up here—and into bed—that much quicker. And talking of which,' he added, rapidly stripping off his dinner-jacket and trousers, 'for pity's sake, hurry up and get your clothes off. It's been six weeks and four days since we last made love—and I warn you that I'm a desperate man!'

'Now that I'm a reformed character, I wouldn't dream of arguing with my husband,' she said primly, but her fingers were trembling so much that he was beside her before she had managed to undo more than half her buttons. *'James!'* she shrieked as he quickly put his hands on either side of the neckline, ripping the garment from top to bottom. 'Do you have any idea how much that dress cost?'

'Do you have any idea of how much I need to make love to you?' he groaned, his voice thick and husky as he quickly tossed aside her underclothes. Urgently drawing her soft body close to him, he covered her face with featherlight kisses before his mouth claimed hers with possessive hunger.

Drowning in ecstasy, Polly surrendered to the magic of his lips and the erotic sensuality of his tongue, her hands moving restlessly down over his body as her fingers blindly retraced the familiar length of his muscled torso; her touch causing the breath to rasp in his throat as he struggled to control his raging ardour. And then their crying need of each other broke through all restraints, her body arching wantonly beneath his, welcoming the hard pressure of his thighs as they parted hers, and the forceful pounding thrusts as he swiftly brought them both to the peak of sexual fulfilment in a raging storm of mutual love and passion.

James was the first to surface from the depths of their explosive consummation. 'My darling, wonderful Polly, there hasn't been a moment of the past weeks when I haven't longed to hold you in my arms,' he murmured softly.

'Hmm...' She snuggled closer to his warm body. 'I missed you dreadfully, as well. When you suddenly turned up this evening at Giles's and Alicia's dinner party, I—well, I simply could hardly believe my eyes! How did you know I was up at the Hall?'

'That's simple—you weren't here, so I reckoned you had to be there.'

'But you were wearing a dinner-jacket. So how...'

He rolled over, trapping her body beneath him. 'I am a master of disguises,' he intoned in dramatic, throbbing tones. 'Superman has nothing on me!'

'I'll second that!' she murmured faintly as his hands began moving erotically over her body. 'Oh, darling, I love you so much,' she whispered, and then there was silence in the room for a long, long time.

'Strewth! I'm going to die young and happy at this rate,' Polly gasped, her eyes dazed with love-making. 'Where on earth do you get all that energy?'

James raised himself up on one elbow and gazed down at her, his fingers gently stroking the soft, burgeoning fullness of her breasts. 'I guess that, as far as your sweet body is concerned, I'm just naturally rapacious.'

'That sounds a nasty complaint. I'd take something for it if I were you,' she teased, her cheeks flushing at being paid such a fabulous compliment.

His shoulders shook with amusement. 'Now, that's what I've been missing. Not just our love-making—superb as it most definitely is—but all the laughs we've shared together,' he said, lowering his head to give her a long, loving kiss. 'There was no way I could get out of the remaining scenes I had to do on location, but I left to come straight here just as soon as I could. He watched the various expressions chasing themselves across her face. 'OK, I think I'd better put you out of your misery straight away, and tell you that Stan McGregor has been hired back again. I and the other guys put in a good word for him, after everyone's tempers had cooled down, and he's happily back at work—and even told me to give you his love.'

'That—that's very kind of him,' she said in a small voice.

'And I've two other bits of good news. Firstly, the film company isn't going to sue me for loss of time on location. It seems that Donald Buckley, the director, has decided to keep the print we did that day in the river, and there will be no difficulty in cutting out your unexpected appearance at the end of the scene. And, secondly, it turns out that Melody's ankle was only a bad sprain, and she's decided not to sue you, me or anyone else she can think of, because—wait for it—she's going to marry Donald Buckley!'

'Is that a good idea?' Polly asked, picking her words carefully.

'Well, it's great for Melody, since it just about guarantees her a place in all her husband's future movies. As for Donald...I don't think the poor chap knows what has hit him, although I can't help feeling he's going to live to regret it,' James said cheerfully.

'I've thought about it an awful lot, and I don't suppose you can really understand why I was so jealous of that awful woman,' Polly said slowly. 'You're used to working with some of the most beautiful girls in the world, and probably get blasé about being surrounded by such fabulous, good-looking women. But, for someone like me, knowing nothing about movies, I couldn't see how you could possibly keep your hands off her! I mean, she may be a ghastly person, but I've never seen anyone so— well, I think "luscious" is about the right word.'

'Actually, the right word is "boring", or maybe "tiresome",' murmured James, clasping her tightly in his arms.

Polly sighed wistfully. 'I wish I was that "boring", she murmured, before finally dismissing Melody Grant from her mind for ever. 'Actually,

it was your films that gave me the hardest time,'
she added. 'I had a long talk to Alicia...'

'Now *there's* a truly beautiful woman. Really
quite lovely,' he said enthusiastically.

'She's also happily married, to a very green-eyed,
vigilant husband!' Polly retorted sharply, before
clicking her teeth at her own folly. 'I refuse to be
jealous of my own stepmother, and besides—you
were just winding me up, weren't you?'

'Yup,' grinned James.

'Well, you can cut it out, right now,' she said
sternly. 'Because I've got quite enough trouble
trying to cope with you on the silver screen, as well
as in my bed... Oh, damn—I'm not putting this
very well,' she groaned. 'I know you can't really
understand the problem, but I asked Alicia how
she'd feel if she went to a movie, and there was
Giles on the screen as large as life—well, larger than
life, in fact and she had to watch him making
mad, passionate love to a really fantastic woman?
And it isn't just me being peculiar, because Alicia
went quite pale at the mere thought! So, please try
to be understanding if I sometimes get a bit twitchy
about it, won't you?'

'Of course I will, sweetheart,' he murmured,
holding her tightly against the hard, muscled wall
of his chest, the strong beat of his heart echoing
hers. 'What you're talking about is, or was, the
real core of the problem between us. For me,
working in the movies is just that—work. I regard
it as a job, no more and no less, and one for which
I am paid an indecently large amount of money.
But that's it. I go through the publicity motions,
of course, because you have to give as well as re-

ceive, but what I really want is a steady home environment. I have a horror of the sort of false, socalled glamorous existence lived by some of my friends, and their children mostly seem to be nasty, spoiled brats. As far as I'm concerned, I can't imagine anything more satisfying than living a simple, quiet life in the country with my wife and children.' He gently brushed the curls away from her brow. 'We got married so quickly—mostly because I wanted to make damn sure of you while I had the chance!—and I never really got around to explaining how I saw our life together. You see, I want us to live here, at Winterfloods, with you carrying on farming as you always have done, and with me going off to work every now and then, but always returning to the quiet, peaceful haven of my own home. I don't want you mixing with the film world, I want to keep our love and our marriage well away from all the frenzied razzmatazz of show business. And I promise you that, in the future, I'm going to make sure that I'm never away for more than a month, or six weeks at the most. How does that sound to you?'

'I'd rather it was only a month, but otherwise that sounds absolutely perfect,' sighed Polly happily.

'Now,' he said, rolling over to stare down into her radiantly happy eyes. 'I know you've got something to tell me, and I think I've been showing remarkable patience, under the circumstances. So— don't you think it's about time you told me about the baby, hmm?'

'Of course I was going to tell you, but in the excitement of . . . *Hang on!*' she exclaimed, jerking herself sharply out of his arms, and gazing stormily at him. 'How did you know about the baby?'

'Calm down,' he said firmly, pulling her back into his arms. 'I'd already arranged my departure for England and bought my ticket some weeks ago. It was only when I met the company doctor in the local bar, the night before I flew out of Malaysia that I learned about your pregnancy. You remember all those tests you had, to see if you were fit enough to fly?' he asked, and when she nodded, he gave a rumble of laughter. 'Well, your tests and others from the various actors went down to a laboratory in Singapore. Now, it's the company's policy to keep a close eye on its female actresses—pregnancy can cause havoc with the shooting schedule. So, being a woman, you got tested along with all the others...and fair enough, as the doctor said when he gave me the good news, since you'd already had a starring role in your first and last film!'

'Don't remind me!' she groaned.

James laughed. 'My poor darling—I'm deeply ashamed of being so nasty and unkind to you after that awful experience you went through.'

'So you should be,' she said, trying to look cross, although her heart wasn't in it. 'Do you . . . are you pleased about the baby?'

'Pleased?' he mouthed the word with distaste. 'What a God-awful, prissy, oh-so-English word to describe the most wonderful thing that has ever happened to me—other than falling in love with you, of course!' he said huskily, drawing her tenderly into his arms, and possessing her lips in a long, rapturous kiss. 'In fact, I thought that I'd get him one of those little Shetland ponies, and teach him to ride just as soon...'

'Him?' she queried with a laugh. 'What if it's a "her"?'

He grinned and shrugged his shoulders. 'Just as long as the baby is healthy, I don't really care what sex it is. Either way, I'm thrilled to bits at the idea of being a father, and who knows—you might even have twins. Now that really would be fantastic fun!'

'I'm not sure about that!' she murmured doubtfully. 'I think one at a time would be a better idea. After all,' she looked at him anxiously, 'I'm not at all sure how you're going to feel about me when I'm heavily pregnant, and staggering around like a hot-air balloon about to explode!'

He laughed. 'What an idiot you are! Of course, I hope we'll have lots of kids, but if you seriously doubt that I'm ever going to lose interest in your delicious body, or the wonderful life we're going to have together, then you aren't the girl I think you are!'

'And what sort of girl do you think I am?' she asked sleepily, smiling happily as he told her at length and in considerable, graphic detail.

'...Not to mention the fact that you're absolutely——' His voice died away as he saw that Polly had fallen sound asleep.

His blue eyes softened with warm tenderness as he gazed down at his beloved wife. He hadn't yet decided whether to tell her about his telephone conversation with Giles Ratcliffe, earlier this morning. 'I want my wife back!' James had said starkly, before asking him how best to achieve a reconciliation with Polly.

After Giles had made it clear that he would personally hang, draw and quarter James if he ever upset Polly again, his advice had been succinct and to the point. 'You'd better meet in company with other people. Otherwise, knowing Polly, she'll either hit you over the head or kick you in the shins. Probably both!' he added with a dry, sardonic laugh. 'So I suggest that your best option is to join our dinner party tonight. Incidentally, I don't propose to tell my wife about our arrangement. Alicia and Polly are quite incapable of keeping secrets from each other,' he had drawled, his voice heavy with amusement. 'And I rather think we don't want to let the cat out of the bag too soon, hmm?'

Giles Ratcliffe was really a very decent guy, James thought, gently brushing the curls from the brow of his sleeping wife. And her stepmother, Alicia, was obviously a kind, sweet woman with a very pretty face—though not nearly as beautiful as his lovely Polly, of course, he thought contentedly, drawing her tenderly into his arms. And, with the complacent smile of a man who is truly blind with love, he too slowly drifted into a deep slumber.

Keepsake

ADULTB-1

Harlequin Presents

Coming Next Month

Available in March wherever paperback books are sold, or through Harlequin Reader Service:

In the U.S.
901 Fuhrmann Blvd.
P.O. Box 1397
Buffalo, N.Y. 14240-1397

In Canada
P.O. Box 603
Fort Erie, Ontario
L2A 5X3

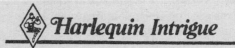

Harlequin Intrigue

Two exciting new stories each month.

Each title mixes a contemporary, sophisticated romance with the surprising twists and turns of a puzzler...romance with "something more."

Because romance can be quite an adventure.

Romance, Suspense and Adventure

**Patricia Matthews, ''America's First Lady of Romance,''
will delight her fans with these spellbinding sagas of
passion and romance, glamour and intrigue.**

Thursday and the Lady A story of a proud and passionate love set during America's most unforgettable era—as suffragettes waged their struggle for the vote, the gold rush spurred glorious optimism and the Civil War loomed on the horizon.	$4.50	☐
Mirrors Intrigue, passion and murder surround a young woman when she learns that she is to inherit an enormous family fortune.	$4.50	☐
Enchanted Caught in the steamy heat of America's New South, a young woman finds herself torn between two brothers—she yearns for one but a dark, foreboding secret binds her to the other.	$3.95	☐
Oasis A spellbinding story chronicling the lives of the movie stars, politicians and rock celebrities who converge at the world-famous addiction clinic in Oasis.	$4.50	☐

Total Amount $ _____
Plus 75¢ Postage   ___.75___
Payment enclosed   _____

Please send a check or money order payable to Worldwide Library.

In U.S.A.	In Canada
Worldwide Library	Worldwide Library
901 Fuhrmann Blvd.	P.O. Box 609
Box 1325	Fort Erie, Ontario
Buffalo, NY 14269-1325	L2A 5X3

Please Print

Name: _____

Address: _____

City: _____

State/Prov: _____

Zip/Postal Code: _____

🌐 **WORLDWIDE LIBRARY**   PAM-1